"Underneath this handsome exterior, I'm a nice guy."

"Oh, sure."

"Give me today and I'll prove you wrong."

"I don't think that's a very good idea, Mackie."

He chuckled. "Providence is on my side." He stepped forward, slid his arm around her waist, pulled her against him, angled his head to one side and settled his lips upon hers. Then his tongue, warm and wet, entered her mouth and leisurely explored. The thrusts gradually went deeper, the strokes became faster, and his mouth grew hungrier. Then he quickly set her away from him.

"Why did you kiss me like that?"

"Curiosity. We've both been thinking about it, right? Ever since yesterday we've both been wondering what it would be like to be together. Now that our curiosity has been satisfied, we can relax around each other and enjoy the day. Right?"

Going along with him would probably end up being a *big* mistake.

Also available from MIRA Books and
SANDRA BROWN
Previously published under the
pseudonym Erin St. Claire
THE DEVIL'S OWN

Coming soon
TWO ALONE

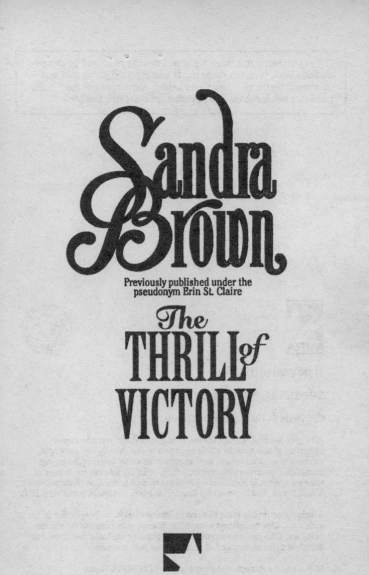

Sandra Brown

Previously published under the
pseudonym Erin St. Claire

The THRILL of VICTORY

MIRA BOOKS

ISBN 1-55166-025-3

THE THRILL OF VICTORY

MIRA and the star colophon are trademarks of MIRA Books.

Printed in U.S.A.

The
THRILL of
VICTORY

Prologue

―❦❦❦―

"Ramsey is out for your butt, Mackie."

The gopher, who had met the star sports-writer of the *Dallas Tribune* at the elevator, fell into step behind him as he walked toward the city room of Dallas' largest newspaper. Judd Mackie was unfazed by the threat of being out of favor with the *Tribune*'s managing editor. He made a beeline for the coffee machine. Its brew was so viscous, so black, he'd often joked that they used the leftovers to fill in the cracks on North Central Expressway.

"Mackie, did you hear me?"

"I heard you, I heard you, Addison. Got a quarter?"

The pockets of his slacks—expensive, but hopelessly wrinkled—hadn't produced the correct amount of change for the vending machine. He was notorious for never carrying money. It was ludicrous that he was bumming from a guy whose age and income were a fraction of his.

"Ramsey's fit to be tied," the gopher said in an ominous undertone as he passed his idol a handful of coins.

"He usually is." Mackie watched a Styrofoam cup fill with coffee whose only virtue was that it was scalding and as darkly opaque as the sunglasses he still had on, though he'd been inside the building a full five minutes.

As he sipped barely diluted caffeine from the disposable cup, the lenses of his glasses fogged over, reminding him they were there. He took them off and dropped them into the breast pocket of his jacket, which wasn't any more dapper than his slacks. His eyelids were puffy; the whites of his eyes were rivered with red.

"He told me to catch you at the elevator and personally escort you to his office."

"He must really be steamed. What'd I do this time?" Judd asked with disinterest. Michael Ramsey was perpetually steamed at him. From one day to the next the extent of his wrath was only a matter of degree.

"I'll let him tell you. You coming peaceably?" the gopher asked worriedly.

Judd took pity on him. "Lead on."

Addison Somethingorother was an intern who worked part-time between his journalism classes at Southern Methodist University. During the boy's first day on the job, Judd had passed him a rumpled handkerchief he'd fished from an even more rumpled pocket and jokingly suggested that the eager student use it to dry behind his ears. But when Addison had looked wounded, Judd had slapped him on the back, said he'd meant no offense, and offered the best advice he could give someone who aspired to a journalistic career, which was to reconsider.

"The hours are long, the pay lousy, the working conditions abysmal and the best you can hope for is that whatever you've written gets read before the dog chews it up or the bird craps on it or the housewife wraps chicken guts in it."

Addison was still around, so apparently he hadn't taken the jaded sports reporter's words to heart. Judd would have continued to rebuke Addison's idealism if he hadn't remembered a time when he himself had had stars in his eyes about a career.

The stars had gone out long ago, but on occasion, usually when he was deep into his cups, he remembered what it felt like to have a burning ambition for greatness. So he let the cub go on dreaming his dreams. He'd find out for himself that life played dirty tricks.

It was midmorning and the city room was a beehive of activity. Reporters at word-processing terminals clicked away on their keyboards. Some had telephone receivers tucked beneath their chins. Messengers hustled among the desks, which were already stacked with packages and mail as yet unopened.

Then there were those individuals simply hanging out, smoking, sipping canned drinks or coffee, waiting for something newsworthy to happen or, short of that, divine inspiration.

". . . the Arabs. But then Israel—hi, Judd— wouldn't do . . ."

"So I said to her, 'Look I want my keys back.' Hi, Judd. To which she said . . ."

". . . me a quote. Hi, Judd. Somebody's got to stick his neck out and go on the record about this thing."

Popular with his cohorts, he nodded greetings as he followed Addison through the maze of desks, then down a carpeted hallway toward the managing editor's office.

"There you are," his secretary said in exasperation. "Since we don't have a militia, he was about to send me in search of you. Thanks, Addison. You can get back to whatever you were doing before Mr. Ramsey summoned you."

The gopher seemed reluctant to leave just when the fireworks were about to start. But Ramsey's secretary was almost as indomitable as the boss himself. He ambled away.

"Hi, doll. What's up?" Judd tossed his empty cup into the nearest wastepaper basket. "Pour me a cup of the real stuff, will you?"

Propping her fists on her hips, the secretary asked, "Do I look like a waitress?"

Judd winked and gave her the leisurely, miss-nothing once-over that rarely failed to make points toward a big score. "You look like a million bucks." He sauntered through the connecting door before she could retaliate against either his blatant sexism or ingratiating compliment.

Inside the door, Judd was greeted by the noxious fumes left by the first two of the four packs of cigarettes Michael Ramsey would smoke that day. He had one cigarette smoldering in an ashtray and another in his mouth when Judd strolled in.

"It's about time." His face was florid with rage.

Judd flopped into a leather chair and crossed his ankles in front of him. "For what?"

"Don't get cute with me, Mackie. You've really blown it this time."

Ramsey's secretary came in bearing the requested cup of coffee, brewed in her personal coffee maker. Judd thanked her with a smile and another suggestive glance that she knew, and regretted, was meaningless.

After she withdrew, Ramsey exhaled a veritable thundercloud of acrid smoke. "You missed the biggest tennis story of the year."

Judd burned his tongue on the coffee and choked on a laugh. "Tennis! You're all red in the face over a tennis story? Geez, as high as your blood pressure is, I thought the Cowboys must've declared bankruptcy. What happened, did McEnroe call the line judge a naughty name?"

"Stevie Corbett collapsed during her morning match at Lobo Blanco."

Judd's grin fell. His attention and his mirth were instantly arrested. He held the coffee cup, real china, against his lips and gazed at Ramsey over the patterned rim. Ramsey ground out the cigarette in the ashtray, took a final drag on the one presently in his mouth, then haphazardly flicked the ashes toward the overflowing ceramic bowl on his desk.

"What do you mean collapsed?"

"Well, now that's what we don't know because we didn't have anybody out there covering the story," Ramsey replied sweetly. "Our overpaid, star reporter was sleeping in this morning."

"Cut the sarcasm, alright? So I overslept. Big deal. What'd Miss Corbett do, trip and fall over her braid?"

"No, she didn't trip. Thankfully the photographer showed up even if you didn't. He said she 'collapsed.'"

"Like fainted?"

"Like dropped down and folded up into a little heap on the court."

"Terrible phraseology."

Ramsey's face went darker red. "If you'd been there, you could have phrased it yourself."

"It wasn't necessary for me to be there," Judd said in his own defense. "Corbett was a cinch to beat that Italian girl."

"Well, she didn't. She had to forfeit the match. She's out of the tournament."

"On the heels of her winning the French Open, this one was a shoo-in. She was playing more as a courtesy than anything. I was going to catch some of the more interesting matches this afternoon."

"When you came to terms with your hangover," Ramsey said balefully. "As it is, you missed reporting on Stevie Corbett's collapse in front of a huge hometown crowd that got up early and fought rush-hour traffic to watch her play while you were still tucked in."

"What's the word on the street?"

"Nothing. Her manager read a statement to the press. It amounted to three sentences that don't tell us a damn thing."

"Which hospital is she in?" Judd was already mentally compiling a list of reliable sources in the medical community who would squeal on their own mothers if the money was green enough.

"She isn't."

"Isn't in the hospital?" The adrenaline rushing through his system ebbed. His quick brain applied the brakes and threw everything into reverse. He coughed another rough laugh and took another drink of the coffee he'd set aside and forgotten. "Leave it to you to blow this all out of proportion, Mike. Cute little Stevie probably had a rough night. As I did."

Ramsey shook his head adamantly. "She had to be carried off the court. This was more than a rough night." He pinned Judd to the chair with a hard stare. "You're going to find out what it was ... *before* anyone else does. And you're going to be playing catch-up ball because the story has already been reported on the radio. Didn't you hear it while you were driving in?"

Judd shook his head. "I didn't turn on the radio. Headache."

"Figures. Here." Ramsey took a tin of aspirin out of the lap drawer of his desk and tossed it to his most intuitive, incisive reporter, who also happened to be the most exasperating. He kept the stock of aspirin for Judd alone.

"Take three of them, all of them, whatever it takes to get yourself in shape and on the phone or out beating the bushes, but find out what brought on Stevie Corbett's collapse.'' He jabbed the space between them with his current cigarette. ''I want your story in time for the evening edition.''

Judd glanced at his watch. ''I kinda had this lunch, uh, thing, set up.''

''Cancel.''

''No,'' Judd drawled as he lazily rolled out of the chair, ''that won't be necessary. I'll just call the young lady and move our date to midafternoon. By then I'll have this Corbett story sewn up and ready to go to press.''

At the door, he gave Ramsey a mocking salute. ''You know, Mike, if you don't calm down, you're going to die young.''

He left the door standing open. Everyone in the city room heard Mike Ramsey call Judd a name that flattered neither him nor his mother.

One

"**O**h, my Lord, *you*."

Stevie Corbett slumped against her front door, which she had just pulled open. She was wearing a short kimono-style robe that overlapped across her chest and was tied with a self-belt at her waist. The light green silk looked as cool and fresh as a ripe honeydew melon.

The details of her attire were noticed by the sportswriter, her nemesis, and the last person on earth she wanted to talk to at that moment.

"I thought you were somebody else," she said.

"Obviously. Who's the lucky dog you were expecting?" His voice was heavily spiced with insinuation.

"My doctor is sending over some medication. I thought you were the delivery boy."

"That's what peepholes are for," Judd reminded her, tapping the small round hole in the door.

"I didn't think to look."

"Got your mind on other things, huh?"

She glanced beyond his wide shoulders, hoping for a glimpse of the expected pharmaceutical delivery. "Yes."

"Like making a fool of yourself at Lobo Blanco Tennis Center this morning."

Her eyes snapped back to his. "As usual, Mr. Mackie, your choice of words is inflammatory and incorrect."

"Not from the way I hear it."

"The way you *hear* it? You weren't there?" She drew a sad face. "What a pity. You would have tremendously enjoyed my humiliation."

He smiled and the lines in his tanned face deepened. "I'm graciously volunteering my shoulder for you to cry on. Why don't you invite me in and tell me all about it?"

"Why don't you go straight to hell?" In contrast to her words, her smile was positively angelic. "You can read about my ignominious fall in your competitor's column."

"I don't have a competitor."

"Nor do you have any modesty, or scruples, or talent, or taste."

He whistled. "That tumble you took this morning did nothing to improve your rotten disposition."

"I have a lovely disposition around everybody except you. And why should I? I'm not a hypocrite. Why should I be pleasant to the columnist who writes scathing articles about me?"

"My readership expects me to be acerbic," he said blandly. "My acid wit is my trademark just like this single long, blond braid is yours." He reached out and ran his fingers over the plaited strands, starting at her shoulder and following it down to the curve of her breast.

Stevie slapped his hand away and tossed the heavy, thick braid over her shoulder. "I ducked the press today. How did you slip past?"

"I know who to bribe for home addresses and such. Why are you ducking the press?"

"I don't feel well, Mr. Mackie. I certainly don't feel like swapping insults with you. If I'd known you were on the other side of my door, I certainly would never have opened it. Please leave."

"One question?"

"No."

"Why did you faint?"

"Goodbye."

She slammed the door in his face, almost catching the hem of his jacket in the crack. For a moment, she rested her forehead against the wood. Judd Mackie of all people! Only yesterday his column had made snide mention of her playing in the tournament at Lobo Blanco.

"This writer can only wonder what the fashion-conscious Ms. Corbett, who recently got lucky at the French Open, will wear to dazzle her adoring hometown fans," he had written. "If only her backhand had as much swing as her cute little skirts."

For years, since she'd become a top-seeded player, Mackie had taken potshots like that at her. If she won, he credited luck for the victory. If she lost, he cruelly elaborated on the reasons why.

Sometimes he was painfully correct in his observations. Those were the times she resented his columns most. He never had a charitable word to say about her either as a person or as an athlete.

Lately, however, she hadn't given his poison pen much room to maneuver. She'd been winning—most recently The French Open, which had put her halfway to getting the Grand Slam. Next, Wimbledon. Wimbledon?

Where the very word usually generated expectation and excitement, it now evoked foreboding. Right now, Judd Mackie was the least of her problems.

Absently she laid her hand over her abdomen and headed toward the kitchen to brew herself a cup of tea. Sometimes drinking something warm made her feel better.

No sooner had she filled the kettle again and set it on the heating burner than her doorbell rang again. This time she wisely used the peephole, but saw through it only the distorted, fisheye view of a prescription bottle. She opened the door.

Judd Mackie was still lounging against the doorjamb, idly shaking the brown plastic bottle of pills in front of the peephole.

Stevie uttered an exclamation of outrage and surprise. "How did you manage that?"

"With a five-dollar bill and my sincere promise to hand-deliver the prescription. I passed myself off as your concerned brother."

"And he believed you?"

"I have no idea. He took the money and ran. Smart fellow. *Now* are you going to ask me in?"

Sighing with resignation, she stepped aside. For several moments after the door closed behind him, they stood regarding each other closely. For all the name-calling and backbiting that had gone on between them over the years, this was the first time they'd ever been alone together.

Well, there had been that one time years ago in Stockholm, but they hadn't exactly been alone and Stevie doubted that he even remembered.

He was taller than he looked from a distance, she realized. Their paths often crossed at local sporting or social or charity events. Sometimes he even waved at her from afar, cheerfully waggling his fingers in a smart-alecky manner that never failed to set her teeth on edge.

Perhaps it was his clothing, which could be described as "casual" at best, that made him appear shorter. With him standing this close, however, she was surprised to discover that her eyes were on a level with his collarbone. She hadn't remembered until he removed his sunglasses that his eyes were hazel—heavy on the gray.

She reached for the bottle of pills. He held them above his head of unruly chestnut hair and out of her reach. "Mr. Mackie!"

"Ms. Corbett!"

The teakettle suddenly whistled shrilly as though ending a round on an impasse. She turned on her bare heel and marched toward the kitchen. He followed her through the wide, airy rooms of her condominium.

"Nice place."

"For a writer that's extremely trite," she said, pouring boiling water over the tea bag in the mug. "Would you like some herbal tea and honey?"

He winced with disgust. "How about a Bloody Mary?"

"I'm fresh out of Bloody Marys."

"A Coke?"

"Diet?"

"Fine. Thanks."

She spooned honey into her tea and took a couple of sips before fixing his cold drink. When she passed it to him, he asked, "Tummy ache?"

"No, why?"

"My mother used to make me drink tea whenever I was recovering from a pukey bout with a stomach virus."

"*You* have a mother?"

He sternly lowered one eyebrow. "That had as much sting as that serve that aced Martina last month."

"As I recall you failed to mention that ace in your column, which said that Martina just had an off day."

"You read my column?"

"You watch my matches?"

Smiling with enjoyment over their verbal sparring, he took a drink from his glass and lowered himself onto a bar stool with a bent-wood back. Stevie thrust out her hand. "May I have my pills now, please?"

He scanned the label on the small bottle. "These are pain pills."

"That's right."

"Toothache?"

She bared her front teeth, exposing them for his examination. "Want to see my molars?"

"Your molars look fine from here," he drawled, his eyelids lowering a fraction.

Stevie gave him a contemptuous glance. "The pills?"

"Muscular injury? Tennis elbow? Sprained shoulder? Stress fracture?"

"None of the above. Will you please give me the medicine now and stop behaving like a jerk?" With a shrug, he set the bottle on the bar and slid it across to her. "Thank you."

"You're welcome. You look like you need them."

"How can you tell?"

"Tension around your mouth." He touched one corner of her lips, then the other.

Stevie yanked her head away and quickly turned her back. She filled a small juice glass with tap water and swallowed two tablets. Retrieving her cup of tea, she sat down on the bar stool next to his.

She drank most of her tea in silence. He studied her every move. Obviously the adage that "if you ignored something long enough it would go away" didn't apply to him.

"What are you doing here, Mackie?" she asked wearily.

"I'm on assignment."

"Isn't there a ball game of some sort you could be writing about this afternoon? A golf tournament? Other matches at Lobo Blanco?"

"You're the big sports story of the day, like it or not."

She averted her eyes and muttered beneath her breath, "I don't like it."

Judd set his elbow on the bar and propped his cheek in his hand. "Why did you collapse out there this morning? It couldn't have been the heat. It wasn't that hot."

"No. It was a perfect day for tennis."

"Stay up past your bedtime last night?"

She gave his dishevelment a critical glance, her disapproval coming through loud and clear. "I never carouse the night before a match."

"Might do your game some good if you did," he said with a crooked smile.

Wryly she shook her head. "You're hopeless, Mackie."

"So I've been told."

"Look, I'm very tired. I was on my way to bed when you showed up the first time. Now that I've taken the medication, I'd like to get some rest. Doctor's orders."

"Your doctor recommended bed rest?"

"Yes."

"Hmm," he said, taking a sip of his drink. "That could mean anything. But I guess if you were drying out or going through drug rehab, you'd be hospitalized."

"You think I've been on alcohol or drugs?" she demanded indignantly, her sagging posture improving dramatically.

He leaned closer and, pulling down her lower eyelids, examined her eyes. "Guess not. No dilation. I doubt you're chemically dependent. You've got good skin tones, no needle tracks, clear eyes."

She angled her head away from his touch. "Yours certainly wouldn't stand up to close scrutiny."

Undaunted, he gave the rest of her an appraisal. "No, come to think of it, you look too healthy to be dependent on anything except low cholesterol, high-fiber foods. Get hold of a bad batch of bean curd?"

She dropped her forehead into her palm. "Would you please just go away?" She was disheartened on several counts. Chief among them was that she needed to be with someone right now, anyone, and Judd Mackie was the only one around. As much as it cost her to admit it, his obnoxious presence was preferable to solitude.

"That narrows down the possibilities considerably," he remarked.

"To what?" In spite of herself she was curious to hear his hypothesis.

"Publicity."

"Give me a break," she moaned. "I don't need it."

"Right," he admitted grudgingly, "you're already hyping enough products to keep your face smiling out of magazines and TV screens for years."

Narrowing his eyes, he assessed her through a screen of thick, spiky lashes. "Are you sure you didn't just fake a fainting spell to get out of playing that match?"

"Why would I do something like that?"

"That Italian broad is supposed to be good."

"But I'm better," Stevie staunchly exclaimed.

"You've *been* good," he conceded reluctantly, "but you're getting up there in age. What is it now, thirty-one?"

He had struck a sore spot and she lashed out, "This has been my best year. You know that,

Mackie. I'm on my way to getting a Grand Slam.''

"You've still got to win Wimbledon."

"I won it last year."

"But your younger competition is breathing down your neck, players with a hundred times more talent and stamina."

"I'm noted for my stamina."

"Yeah, yeah, along with your saucy braid. You're not an athlete."

"As much as any football player in the NFL."

"You don't look like an athlete. You're not even built like one."

Stevie, angered over his sneering accusation, followed the direction of his gaze down to her chest. Her robe was gaping open, revealing the smooth, pale slope of one breast. She hurriedly gathered the fabric together in her fist and stood up. "It's past time for me to throw you out."

Unperturbed, he continued smoothly. "Maybe your collapse was brought on by anxiety, pure and simple."

Stevie was seething, but said nothing. She wouldn't honor his ridiculous theories with a response. Her expression remained impassive.

"You've always known, deep down, that you don't have what it takes to be a real champion. You're one bowl of Wheaties short," he said tauntingly. "You're a flash in the pan."

"Hardly that, Mackie. I've been on the pro tour for twelve years."

"But you didn't do anything significant until about five years ago."

"So, I'm improving, not declining, with age."

"Not according to what happened this morning."

"My age has nothing to do with why I—"

He sprang to his feet and bore down on her. "Come on, give, Stevie. Why did you faint?"

"None of your damn business!" she shouted.

"Cramps? Hmm? Is all this hullabaloo over a case of cramps?"

"No! Definitely not cramps."

"Ah." Judd released the word slowly. Tilting his head to one side, he let his eyes slide down her body again, searching for a telltale sign he might have previously missed. "Is there any particular reason why it's 'definitely not cramps'?" he asked in a lilting voice. "Like a b-a-b-y perhaps?"

Her eyes rounded. "You're crazy."

"And you're pregnant," he concluded bluntly. Drawing his face into a stern frown, he demanded, "Whose is it? That Scandinavian cobbler who designed your special tennis shoes?"

"I'm not pregnant."

"Or is the happy father that polo player from Bermuda?"

"It's Brazil!"

"Brazil, then. The guy with all those chains on his chest and at least four dozen teeth."

"Stop right there."

"Or don't you know whose it is?"

"Stop it!" she screamed, folding her arms across her abdomen. "There is no baby!" She repeated it more softly, more tearfully. "There is no baby."

Tears began to roll down her pale cheeks. "And before long there probably won't be anything else there, either. Because when they take out the tumors, they'll probably have to take out everything."

Two

~~~~~~~~~~~~~~~~~~~~~~~~~~~~~~

Her outcry took Judd completely by surprise. He made a little hiccuping sound when he sharply sucked in his breath. It was a reaction foreign to his character, as he was usually indifferent to even the most appalling pieces of information. This was one time he couldn't shrug and go on his uncaring way.

Stevie turned her back on him. The long blond braid hanging down her back no longer looked saucy, as it did swishing behind her on a tennis court. It looked heavy and burdensome. Or was it that she suddenly seemed so small and defenseless?

Her narrow shoulders shook with her sobs. She was crying openly, making heartrending, strangling sounds that penetrated his cynicism and prompted him to touch her.

"Shh, shh." He took those shuddering shoulders between his hands and turned her to face him. Disregarding her resistance, he pulled her against him and wrapped his arms around her. "I'm sorry. If I'd known it was anything that serious, I wouldn't have badgered you."

He doubted that she would believe him. He could hardly believe himself. He rarely apologized for anything. Almost never to a woman.

For a woman sobbing her heart out, all he usually felt was contempt and impatience to escape her clutching hands. But when Stevie Corbett's fingers curled inward toward his chest in a silent plea for help and support, it didn't occur to him to get the hell out before coming involved. Instead he drew her closer and turned his head, resting his cheek on the crown of her blond hair.

He held her while she cried. That in itself was an oddity. When he held a woman, it was strictly for prurient purposes. When he held one wearing a short kimono that did great things for her bare legs, they were as good as in bed. When he held one wearing a short kimono with nothing underneath it except panties, his hands were usually inside it, not stroking her back consolingly.

Those comparisons no doubt accounted for how differently this embrace felt from any other in his recent, or even distant, memory.

His trained eye would have had to go blind to miss the details of her bralessness, the attraction of her smooth thighs, the delightful faint outline of bikini panties beneath the robe, but he didn't follow through on any sexual impulses.

To do so would have made him a real heel. He *was* a heel, but so far, he hadn't stooped that low. Or maybe guilt was keeping his caresses platonic and circumspect. After all, he'd unwittingly induced this emotional breakdown. Unlike the other women he had reduced to tears during his career as a bastard, Stevie Corbett had a helluva good reason for needing to cry.

Eventually her sobs turned into soft, catchy, moist little breaths that he felt through the cloth of his shirt. "Shouldn't you be in bed?" he asked softly.

She nodded and stepped away from him, making ineffectual swipes at her eyes. They were still leaking tears and leaving muddy mascara trails down her cheeks.

He had a hot broad waiting to feed him a cold lunch. Mentally he kissed them both goodbye. Surprising himself even more than he surprised Stevie, he bent slightly at the knees and lifted her into his arms.

"This isn't necessary, Mackie. I can walk."

"Which way?"

She hesitated, then raised her arm and pointed. She had great muscle tone, which at any other time would have warranted leisurely exploration with fingertips and lips. On the other hand, she was so light that he could carry her for a hundred miles and not break a sweat, at least not from exertion. Holding her against him for any extended period of time without doing anything about it might make him perspire.

"In there."

He carried her into a spacious bedroom filled with natural light and an overabundance of potted plants. "Didn't they film a Tarzan movie here once?" he wisecracked.

"These plants are my pets. It's cheaper to have them taken care of while I'm away than it is to board a dog or cat. Besides, they can't miss me."

He deposited her on the edge of the bed. "Lie down."

"I'll bet you say that to all the girls," she remarked drolly.

"I'm not kidding around. And neither should you be. Lie down."

She reclined on the heap of eyelet-covered pillows. By her expression, Judd knew it felt good to her, though she'd probably never admit it.

"Sorry about your shirt."

"Huh?" He glanced down and noticed that it was damp and smudged with makeup. "It'll wash," he said negligently.

He shook out a light, puffy, quilted comforter, which was folded at the foot of the bed, and covered her with it. He then sat down on the edge of the mattress, his hips even with hers.

"Talk."

"Not to you, Mackie."

"My name is Judd."

"I know that. I've seen it on your byline."

"Forget the column for a minute, will you?"

"Have you?" she shot up at him.

"Yes!"

During the ensuing silence, he watched tears fill her eyes again—light brown eyes the color of very expensive scotch. "Stevie," he said gently, "this is off-the-record. I think you need to talk to someone."

"Yes, I do, but..." She sniffed wetly; he popped a Kleenex out of the box on the nightstand and held it to her nose.

"Blow." She did. He tossed that Kleenex in the wastebasket and used a fresh one to dab at her eyes. "You need a sounding board, right?"

"I just don't feel natural talking to you like this."

"Well," he said, shaking his head ruefully, "this is a highly unnatural situation for me, too. Usually when I'm on a bed with a half-naked broad, the last thing on my mind is conversation. And she would be using her mouth for something besides spilling out her problems."

"Mackie!"

"Judd. Now talk. When did you find out about these tumors?"

"This morning," she said huskily.

"Before your match?" She nodded. "Whose bright idea was it to tell you before a match?"

"Mine."

"Figures."

She frowned up at him. "I'd had some tests done. I wanted to know the results. *Had* to know."

Her gaze drifted to the window where a box of paperwhites were blooming on the sill. "I guess I wasn't really expecting the worst, though. I'd told myself I was prepared to hear it, but..." She looked back at him. "You were right. I collapsed from anxiety."

"Justifiably so."

He rubbed his hands together, studying them intently, as though he'd never noticed his blunt nails, the sprinkling of hair across the backs of his knuckles, the thick wrists that should have belonged to a professional baseball player and didn't.

"These tumors, they're, uh . . ."

"On my female organs," she told him, glancing away again. "I'd been having some pain, more than ordinary."

He cleared his throat uncomfortably. He was learning that where the female body was concerned, he had a teenage boy's mentality. He liked to look and touch and have sex with it. He thought the variations among individual women were intriguing and considered himself a connoisseur of the finest. He had never been faithful to one in particular. He had enjoyed more than his fair share of them, more than he was proud to admit in this age of safe sex.

Yet, this was the first time he'd ever thought of a female body from an objective standpoint. He considered what it meant to the owner instead of what it meant to him. It contained a person. It wasn't just a soft, beautiful instrument of pleasure.

He didn't like himself very much at that moment and would have found it hard to meet his own eyes in a mirror.

"So they're going to operate and take them out," she was telling him softly. "It'll take months for me to recover and regain my strength, *if* the tumors are benign."

"You mean they might not be?"

"No, they might not be." They shared a long stare, a heavy, ponderous stare full of implication.

"But there's a good chance they are," Stevie continued briskly. "If that's the case, the surgery can be delayed until a more convenient time. Either way, they'll probably have to do a complete hysterectomy."

Judd came to his feet and began pacing the length of the bed. He glanced down at her angrily. "Why in hell are you lying on your butt here? Why aren't you in the hospital and on your way to the operating room?"

"I can't have surgery now," she exclaimed. "Wimbledon is barely a month away."

"So?"

Her lips narrowed with vexation over his obtuseness. "So I've got to play."

"It's not going anywhere. There's always next year."

"As you so unkindly pointed out earlier, I'm not getting any younger. I'm playing better than ever, but for how long?"

Shaking her head adamantly, she continued. "This is my year. My time. If I don't get that Grand Slam now, I'll never have another opportunity, no matter what the surgeons find when they operate. Maybe, if I were ten years younger, I could come back. As it is, it would take months, possibly longer. Even then, I'd never be as strong as I am now."

"What if those tumors are malignant?"

"Naturally that makes things more complicated," she replied evasively.

"How complicated?" She refused to answer. Testily he repeated, "How complicated?"

"If they're malignant, delaying surgery for several weeks could be fatal."

Judd propped his fists on his hips and looked down at her with consternation. "You're crazy, lady."

"You can't judge me because you don't know what you'd do in this situation."

"Does your gynecologist have an opinion?"

"He wants to do the surgery immediately, but he says two weeks won't make much difference."

"Immediately gets my vote."

"You don't get a vote."

"What about your manager?"

"He sees both sides and has left the decision strictly up to me. But he says if I play Wimbledon, I can only have two weeks to make up my mind."

"Meanwhile, you're in pain."

"It's not constant. It comes and goes. Naturally he wants what's best for me."

"He wants what's best for his business interests in you."

"That's unfair."

"What about your parents?"

"They're deceased."

"Lovers?"

"There's no one else to consult." She glared up at him. "Not the 'Scandinavian cobbler' who, by the way, happens to be approaching seventy and has countless grandchildren."

"What about the bare-chested Brazilian with the Ipana smile?"

"I loathe that lecher. Whoever leaked the story of our so-called affair must have graduated from the same school of yellow journalism that you did."

He ignored the gibe. "So you're all alone in this."

"Until you splash it across the sports page. Then everybody will know and have an opinion."

"This conversation is off-the-record, remember?"

"I just wondered if you did."

"I won't print the story, but it'll get out the minute you check into the hospital."

"I'm not sure when that will be."

"Yeah? Well I think you're nuts for not having this taken care of pronto."

"Have you ever had surgery, Mr. Mackie?"

He hesitated before answering. "Not abdominal surgery."

"Then who are you to be giving me advice? Unsolicited advice, I might add."

"Look," he said impatiently, "you're not just screwing around with a career here. We're talking about your *life*."

"Tennis is my life."

"Now who's being trite?"

She tossed her head and gave him a lofty glance. "I've got a lot to think about, Mr. Mackie, and you're a disruptive element. Now that you've got the sensational story you came after, kindly leave."

"Okay. Maybe I'll go back to my office and start working on your obit."

She sprang into a sitting position. The comforter slid to her waist. "You can't possibly understand how difficult a decision this is for me."

"Life and death? That's a difficult decision?"

"It's hardly that simple. I don't know that the tumors are malignant. I don't know that delaying the surgery will be fatal. What I *do* know is that if I have an operation now, my career will be over. That's the only certainty I've got right now and the only one I can base my decision on.''

She pulled in a deep breath, a reloading procedure as it were. ''You can't judge me, Mackie, because you've never had to sacrifice your life's dream. Your dreams don't extend beyond the next easy woman and double highball.''

He couldn't argue with her observation since it so accurately described the life he was currently leading, but it made him mad as hell that she'd pegged him correctly. Intentionally or not, she had vocalized his secret opinion of himself. He couldn't deny her allegations. He wasn't about to leave, however, without getting in a parting shot.

''Before I go, there's something you probably should know, Miss Corbett.''

''Well?'' she demanded.

''Your robe is open.''

''Yes, I'm feeling much better, thank you.''

It was hours later and Stevie was speaking with her gynecologist by telephone. ''The medication helped relax me. I took a long nap.''

Her sleep had been interrupted only by dreams of Judd Mackie's handsome, leering face, looking exactly as it had when he had nodded down at her chest and called attention to her exposed breasts. He was despicable and she rightfully despised him.

"It was just a silly fainting spell, brought on by anxiety over the test results."

The doctor took issue with her blasé attitude and urged her to let him schedule surgery right away.

"You agreed, doctor, that two weeks wouldn't be critical one way or another," she reminded him. "I need that much time to weigh my options and think this through."

She hung up moments later. He had urged her to seek a second opinion. She didn't tell him she already had. And a third. The tumors were definitely there on her uterus and ovaries. Whether or not they were malignant could only be determined by surgery.

On that dismal thought, Stevie padded into the living room and switched on the television. She was just in time to catch the sportscast on the local evening news. There she was, sprawled on the green tennis court like a rag doll while the hushed crowd looked on.

Her collapse had resulted in a mad scrambling of media and tournament officials. Blessedly she'd been unconscious during the mayhem. She didn't remember anything after walking onto the court, wondering if that tournament would be her last.

At the time of her collapse, she'd had her opponent down by two games. Her playing must have been instinctual, mechanical. She remembered nothing of it.

" . . . can only speculate on the nature of Ms. Corbett's illness," the sportscaster was saying. "A statement issued by her manager merely stated that her condition isn't serious and that she is resting in an undisclosed location. And now we're going live to Ranger Stadium where the—"

She switched off the set flippantly, "A few tumors. Nothing serious. My career will probably come to an end, and I'll never be able to have children, but it's really nothing at all."

She went into the kitchen, more out of habit than because she was actually hungry. Spying the glass that Judd Mackie had drunk from, she placed it in the dishwasher. "Out of sight, out of mind."

But he wasn't out of mind, and that was galling. He was very much on her mind. Why? Perhaps because she hadn't expected him to treat her so kindly when she started crying. Or maybe because she'd won his promise not to leak her story. She supposed that when she did make a final decision, she should call him with the story first. For behaving so honorably today, he deserved that consideration.

She ate a bowl of granola and fresh strawberries—out of spite for his sardonic comment about her healthy diet—and retired again to her bedroom.

Unplaiting her braid, she was again reminded of Judd. He'd touched her hair, the corners of her lips. He'd held her in his arms, apparently in no hurry for her to stop crying.

He had even carried her in his arms. It disturbed her that she could so clearly remember the feel of his sleeve against the backs of her bare thighs and the strength of his chest beneath her rib cage.

He was her mortal enemy who constantly attacked her with his vicious pen. Yet, now that she was alone and no one could read her mind, she confessed that his touch had elicited unexpected physical reactions: a fluttering in her breasts, a tightening in her belly, a sensation of swelling and fever between her thighs.

Slouching on the bar stool in her kitchen, he had looked rumpled and crumpled and comfortable. His dark brown hair was worn long, not because he consciously chose a longer style but because he neglected to have it cut regularly.

He was attractive in a disheveled, disreputable, range-wolf way. Debonair he was not. But he was sexy. The chip he carried on his shoulder only added to his appeal. So did his arrogance. To a woman with sensitivity, he would be lethal. Stevie pitied any who might fall in love with Judd Mackie.

As she brushed out her hair, she chided herself for letting him arouse her temper. She had been foolish to engage in a shouting match with him. No one could understand her dilemma, especially not him. What did he know of denied ambitions? He'd never had aspirations to rise above the level of mediocrity. He was an elegant bum, content with half measures.

One thing he did know was women, Stevie conceded. He had known that his departing line would be a zinger she wouldn't easily forget.

She finished brushing her hair and got into bed. She slept on her side because lying on her back and pulling her stomach taut often caused her discomfort. Stacking her hands beneath her cheek, she stared beyond the hem of her pillowcase into the darkened room and thought about Judd. Involuntarily she recalled the drowsy appraisal he'd given her breasts. Had he noticed that her silk kimono had deliciously abraded her nipples to tautness?

Even as she fell asleep, she was blushing over the possibility that he had.

Three

"Hello," Judd mumbled into his telephone. "This better be damned important," he added after consulting the digital clock on his nightstand.

"Oh, it is, it is."

"Mike, for godsake, why're you calling so early?"

"To fire you."

Exasperated, Judd blew out a gust of breath and buried his head back into the pillow. "You did that already last week."

"This time it sticks."

"You say that every time."

"You lazy, no-account bastard, I mean it this time. Have you seen the morning papers?"

"I haven't even seen the morning."

"Well, let me be the first to inform you that your competitor got the story you were supposed to get and didn't."

"Huh?"

"While you were clacking out that less-than-inspiring piece about the Rangers' new Mexican rookie catcher, our friends over at the *Morning News* were scooping you about Stevie Corbett. She's got cancer."

Judd swung his legs over the side of the bed, cursing the twisted sheets that restrained him, and damning his splintering headache and furry mouth. He and some cronies had gone to a topless joint after the Ranger game the night before. There'd been a lot of beer and a lot of bare breasts. He had swilled down beer after beer, in the vain hope that out of the plethora of bobbing breasts he would see something as sexily enticing as an angry Stevie Corbett with her robe gaping open. He hadn't, so he'd kept drinking.

"What the hell are you talking about, Mike? And you don't have to shout."

"I thought you said you talked to Corbett yesterday."

"I did."

"You also said there was no story there."

"In my opinion there wasn't."

"You don't think the fact she's got ovarian cancer is a story?" the editor bellowed.

"She doesn't have cancer!" Judd shouted right back, though it intensified his headache. "She's got a few tumors that might or might not be malignant. How'd they find out about it over at the *News*?"

For the span of several seconds there was a taut silence. Judd didn't notice. He had left the bed and carried the cordless phone into the bathroom with him. His reflection in the mirror over the basin confirmed what his headache had already suggested: the night before had been a bitch.

"You knew about this? You *knew*?" Mike Ramsey roared. "And you gave me tripe for last night's edition?"

Judd didn't have to hold the telephone against his ear to hear the forthcoming tirade. He had it memorized anyway. So he propped the instrument on the edge of his bathroom sink and commenced to shave.

"You're no journalist," Mike shouted over the sound of running water. "You wouldn't even have a column if you didn't carouse in the taverns where players and fans hang out. You're not a reporter, you're a stenographer. All you do is regurgitate boozy conversations and call it creative journalism."

Judd had finished shaving. He picked up the phone long enough to sputter through a mouthful of toothpaste foam, "The readers eat it like candy, lap it up like ice cream. What would your sports page be without my column? Nothing, Ramsey, and you know it."

"I'm willing to find out what it would be. You've just written your last column for me. You got that, Mackie?"

"Yeah, yeah."

"I mean it this time. You're fired! I'll have Addison clean out that rat's nest you call a desk. You can pick up the contents at the receptionist's desk on the first floor. Don't let me see your booze-bloated face in the city room again."

The next sound coming from the telephone was a dial tone. Unperturbed, Judd stepped into the shower. Before he got out, he'd already forgotten Ramsey's call. He got fired half a dozen times a month. It never stuck.

Even if it did, it might be the best thing that could happen to him. Because Ramsey was right in one respect: his column *was* just transcriptions of what he overheard after sporting events, garnished with a few witticisms that didn't tax his imagination any longer than it took him to type them. For the past year or so, he'd been telling himself that his readers didn't know his column came that easily for him and that it wouldn't matter to them if they did.

But it mattered to him. He knew that what he was writing wasn't worth the paper it was printed on. He was grossly overpaid for the amount of work required of him to produce the daily column. Fooling his editor, the man who signed his paycheck, and his reading audience no longer gave him any satisfaction. It got harder each day to laugh up his sleeve about it.

That's why he boozed it up and slept with women he didn't care about and let the days of his life tick by without anything to show for them. He had nothing to care about, nothing to work toward, nothing to get up in the morning for. His life was a big fat zero in the productivity department. Even though he was the only one who realized it, the fact was hard to live with.

He needed a creative challenge, but was afraid that whatever literary talent he had once possessed had been squandered, never to be re-gained. So what? He was too old now to think seriously about a career change.

His future, however, wasn't his main concern right now. Stevie Corbett's was. Where had his rival columnist heard about her illness? And how did she feel about the most intimate aspects of her life providing fodder for the sports page?

It didn't take him long to find out.

She exhibited her famous forehand, aiming the tennis racquet directly at his head.

"What the—"

"You bastard!"

He had ducked her first swing at him, then caught the handle of the racquet as she executed an arcing backhand. They wrestled over the racquet. "What the hell's wrong with you?" he shouted.

"You leaked the story. You told me our conversation was off-the-record. You liar! You—"

"I did no such thing."

"Oh, yes you did," she ground out. "You were the only one who knew."

He yanked the racquet out of her hands and threw it to the floor. "Do you think I'd feed the story to my competition? *I* didn't write the piece.

It was printed in another newspaper. I haven't even read the damn article yet."

Stevie curbed her frustration and fury and thought about that for a second. Why would he give the story to someone else? It didn't make sense. But not much in her life did these days.

"Then how did you know about the article?" she asked suspiciously. "And how did you get past the police?"

Since early morning, her yard had been crawling with reporters. Her manager had finally called the police, requesting that they cordon off her condominium.

"One of the patrolmen on duty owed me a favor."

"For what?"

"It has to do with his sister."

She rubbed her forehead. "I don't think I want to know."

"I don't think you do, either. Suffice it to say she sneaked into a locker room one night after a big game and served as hostess for a spontaneous victory celebration."

Stevie stared up at him, shaking her head in dismay. "I believe you. Why would you make up such a sordid tale?"

He took her by the shoulders and guided her back onto the bar stool in the kitchen, where she'd been sitting when he picked the lock on her back door and slipped through. That's when she had begun hurling insults at him and taking well-placed swats at his head with the racquet she had helped design.

"How did that columnist find out about me, Mackie?"

"I don't know. But I intend to learn." He reached for her kitchen extension and punched out a number. He asked for the sportswriter by name. Apparently they were friendly rivals.

"Hey, Mackie here. Congrats on your story about the Corbett broad." Stevie shot him a fulminating look, which he ignored. "How'd you manage to sweet-talk her into revealing the intimate details of her life? Or should a gentleman ask?" Stevie's mouth dropped open. Judd covered it with his hand. "Oh, no? She didn't tell you? Hmm. Her manager maybe?"

Stevie shoved his hand away from her mouth and adamantly shook her head.

"Okay, I give. Uncle. Who talked? Come on, the cat's already out of the bag so you might as well tell me." Stevie watched his brows pull together into a steep frown. "Look, you ornery cuss, I busted my buns yesterday trying to track down the reason for her collapse and came up empty. Just tell me who I missed."

He listened for a moment. His frown smoothed out, but he didn't look any happier. "I see. Well, you pulled a fast one on me this time, pal. Don't let it happen again." She overheard the vulgarity that was offered in a friendly, harmless manner. "Same to you. Have a nice day," Judd finished in a singsong voice.

"Well?" she asked as he replaced the receiver.

"A technician at Mitchell Laboratories."

"Where I had the sonargram done," she wailed softly. "I knew no one in my doctor's office would talk. I never thought of someone at the lab."

"Don't be naive. Anybody'll talk if you bait the trap right. Coffee cups?"

"Second cabinet, second shelf."

"Want some?"

"No thanks. I've had plenty."

He poured himself a cup and carried it back with him to the bar. He sat down on the bar stool beside her, exactly as they'd been the day before.

"How'd you sleep?" he asked.

"Fine."

"The circles under your eyes say otherwise."

She had avoided looking directly at him for fear that he'd see she hadn't slept well at all. The truth was that she'd had a very restless night filled with dreams that fluctuated from strange to erotic to terrifying. He'd played a rolle in all of them. She was exhausted. But it irked her that he had so tactlessly pointed out how bad she looked.

"Well you look worse for wear, too," she retaliated snidely.

"It was a helluvan evening."

"Then what are you doing here? Why aren't you wherever you call home sleeping it off? Or did you come to gloat?"

She noted the tensing around his mouth, indicating his irritation, but he calmly sipped his coffee. "I might be gloating if I'd written the article. I didn't. If I had, I would have gotten the facts straight."

The starch went out of her then. Gloomily she said, "The way this article reads, I'm finished as a player, and all but dead and buried."

Judd came off the stool so quickly and cursed so viciously that she started in reaction. "Don't say anything like that again. It gives me the creeps."

"Well, I'm sorry I offended your sensibilities," she snapped. "But they happen to be my tumors and I'll talk about them any way I damn well please. If you don't like it, you can leave. Which isn't a bad idea."

It *was* a bad idea. The idea of his leaving didn't appeal to her at all. Now that she knew he was innocent of the crime and no longer felt like murdering him, she was really glad to have him around. At least when he was with her, she had to keep her mental reflexes sharpened. That exercised her mind and kept it from dwelling on dismal thoughts.

To safeguard against his knowing how badly she wanted him to stay, she assumed an aloof and hostile expression. "There's nothing you can do here except further aggravate me, so you might just as well go."

"I came to drive you to the hospital."

"I'm not going to the hospital. I told you that yesterday. I've got two weeks—"

"Look, Stevie—"

"No, *you* look, Mackie. This is my life, my decision, and nobody—"

The doorbell rang. "Ms. Corbett!" Someone began shouting through the door. "How do you feel about having cancer and giving up professional tennis?"

"Oh," she cried, "why don't they leave me alone?" Nerves already frazzled, she ducked her head and covered it with her arms.

Eventually the persistent reporter gave up or was hauled away by one of the policemen who were supposed to be guarding against such intrusions. The house fell silent again. She flinched when Judd laid his hands on her shoulders.

"At least let me get you away from here for a few hours." He swiveled her bar stool around, separating his legs and positioning her knees between them.

"Why would you want to do that?"

"To make up for being such a jackal and sniffing out blood yesterday."

"But you didn't write the story."

"In a way, though, I still feel responsible." She made a scoffing sound. "I know you think I'm a sorry excuse for a journalist," he said, "just like I think you're a sorry excuse for an athlete.

I drink too much, party too hard and have a great capacity for self-indulgence. I'm unreliable and sarcastic. But basically, underneath this ruggedly handsome exterior, I'm a nice guy."

"Oh, sure."

His face broke into a roguish grin that made her tummy flutter. "Give me today and I'll prove you wrong."

She wanted to consent, but hesitated. For all his charm, he might still be working on a story about her. Maybe he was planning an in-depth character profile that would portray her as the shallow "deb of the tennis courts," as he had once dubbed her.

"I don't think that's a very good idea, Mackie. I'll take my chances here."

Almost simultaneously her telephone started ringing and the doorbell pealed again. "Did you plan that?" she accused.

He chuckled, delighted with those unexpected endorsements of his idea. "Providence is on my side. Go get whatever you might need during the day. We won't be back until after dark tonight." The instructions were given as though the matter had been settled to his satisfaction.

"Mackie, even if I wanted to spend the day out on the town with you, which I don't, it wouldn't work anyway. We're both too well-known. We couldn't go anywhere in the city without being recognized and hounded."

"That's why we're going *out* of the city."

"Out of the city? Where?"

"You'll see."

"How do you plan to sneak past all those reporters?"

"Will you quit stalling and go get your things?" he asked impatiently.

Stevie warily studied his face. It looked no more trustworthy than a pirate's. They would probably spend the day quarreling. But the alternative of being held under siege in her own house was even more gruesome.

Mind made up, she spread wide the short skirt of her white cotton culottes, which she had on with a T-shirt and sandals. "Can I go like this?"

"Sure can. Get your purse."

In under five minutes, she reentered the kitchen carrying a canvas tote bag into which she had stuffed everything she might conceivably need. Judd was at the sink, rinsing out the coffeepot.

"You make yourself right at home, don't you?"

"Hmm." He unhurriedly dried his hands on a dish towel, then tossed it aside. "I do."

He stepped forward, slid his arms around her waist, pulled her against him, angled his head to one side and settled his lips upon hers.

Stevie was caught so totally unaware that she didn't put up a struggle or utter a single sound of protest. He kissed her lightly, gently bouncing his lips against hers, until they rested there.

On its way up to her neck, his hand grazed her breast. It brushed against the tip and caused it to bead. His touch couldn't even be counted as a bonafide caress, but Stevie's reaction was very real. A sudden infusion of heat spread through her middle. Its intensity heightened when he re-adjusted their bodies, fitting his into the notch of her thighs.

As his fingers closed around her neck, his tongue playfully probed at the seam of her lips, lazily, halfheartedly, as though he didn't give a damn whether she parted them or not. If she did, fine. He would kiss her. If not, fine. He would be amused, not angry or disappointed.

Stevie parted them.

Then his tongue, warm and wet, entered her mouth and leisurely explored. At least the kiss started off leisurely. The change came on so gradually that it wasn't noticeable until the thrusts of his tongue went deeper, the strokes became faster, and the suction of his mouth grew hungrier. The whole character of the kiss altered. Likewise, so did their responses to it.

When Judd's response became so obvious it could be felt through their clothing, he quickly set her away. She gazed up at him with a mix of desire and bewilderment.

"Why did you kiss me like that?"

"Curiosity." He croaked the word, cleared his throat and repeated it. "We've both been thinking about it, right? Ever since I saw your breasts yesterday, we've been wondering what it would be like to be together. Now that our curiosity has been satisfied, we can relax around each other and enjoy the day. Right?"

Stevie knew that if she became anymore relaxed, she would melt into a puddle of wanting woman on the kitchen floor. But she nodded wordlessly.

Going along with this idea of his would probably end up being a big mistake.

Four

❧❧❧

"You missed your calling." They were underway. Stevie spoke to him over the thrum of his sports car's engine as he weaved it through traffic. "You should have been a criminal."

His plan of escape had called for her to create a diversion at the front door of her condominium by poking her head outside just long enough for the reporters and film crews to think she might be prepared to give them a statement. Then while they were clambering across her lawn toward the entrance, Judd and she had slipped out the back, jogged down the alley and, undetected, got into his car, which he'd left parked on the next street.

"I thought about going into grand larceny," he said expansively, "but figured that it required too much ambition and hard work."

Smiling, Stevie settled comfortably into the leather upholstery. The moment they had left her condominium, a sense of freedom had stolen over her. The break from her normal disciplined routine was in itself a luxury. Most mornings by this time, she had already put in hours of physical conditioning and practice. She remarked on her delinquency to Judd.

"When did you start playing tennis?" Glancing over his shoulder to make sure the lanc was clear, he took a ramp onto the interstate highway and headed east, leaving Dallas behind.

"I was twelve."

"Late for most players who get as far as you have," he observed.

"A little, but I can hardly remember a time when I haven't intimately known the feel of a racquet in my hand." She thought back to the night she had first expressed an interest in playing the sport. "Out of the blue, I told my parents that I wanted to try out for the junior-high tennis team." She had made that startling announcement over supper. "Mother and Daddy looked at me as though I'd said I wanted to move to Mars.''

"Tennis?"

"Yes, sir."

"That's a rich kid's sport," her father had said, returning to his meal. *"Pass the potatoes."*

"What did they have against tennis?" Judd asked.

"Nothing really. It's just that they couldn't relate to it. My mother had no interest in athletics whatsoever. Daddy only liked sports like football and basketball and, of course, those were for boys."

She had been an only child, a *female* only child, who knew that her gender was a vast disappointment to the gruff stranger she called Daddy.

"So how did you get their permission to play?"

"After dinner, I broached the subject with Mother while we were doing the dishes. I explained that the school had racquets and balls I could use. I wouldn't have to buy anything. She said okay."

Stevie went on to tell Judd that by the time she reached high school she had a passion for the sport. She saved baby-sitting money to finance the lessons she took at an exclusive club in north Dallas.

"We weren't members. Any member's bar bill might exceed what my dad earned in a month." There was no rancor in her tone. She'd never been bitter over her family's modest economic level, only impatient with her parents' disinclination to improve it.

"I was playing in a tournament on the club team when I met Presley Foster."

"You're wearing your shoes a size too large. Your backhand stinks and your forehand isn't much better, though you've got good, basic strokes. You show off for the spectators more than you concentrate on your strategy. If you get two points behind, you automatically sacrifice the game. Your serves are hard and fast, but inconsistently so. You don't put forth any effort unless you have to, and that's a damn bad habit to get into."

She paraphrased Presley Foster's first words to her. Judd whistled. "Geez."

She could look back on it now and laugh. "I felt like all but the very top of my head had been hammered into the ground. Then he said, 'But you've got talent. I can refine it, make you a world-class player. You'll hate me before we're finished. I need two years.' ''

One week after her high-school graduation, she had left with the famous coach for his camp in Florida. Her decision had been incomprehensible to her parents. Tennis was no job. Tennis was a game. She went despite their objections. She might have no future in tennis, but she certainly had none by staying at home and stagnating with them.

"I didn't know what hard work was until I came under Presley's tutelage," she told Judd with a wry smile.

She had been dreadfully outclassed by the players who had begun tournament training in grade school and had attended Foster's tennis summer camps. Most of them had played tennis to the exclusion of everything else. Some had had no childhood at all. Tennis was everything.

"I was nineteen before I went on the circuit." She gazed out the window at the landscape whizzing by. Judd drove competently, but fast. "I was playing a tournament in Savannah, Georgia, when I received word that my parents' house had been destroyed by a tornado and they'd been killed.''

"They died in that storm? The one that tore up half of east Dallas?"

"Yes. Practically the whole neighborhood was destroyed. I was lying face down on my bed in the motel room in Savannah, crying, when Presley stormed in and demanded to know why I wasn't on the court warming up for my scheduled match."

"My parents are dead. You don't expect me to play today, do you?"

"I damn sure do! It's times like this that a player shows the stuff she's made of."

She had played. She had won. She'd flown to Dallas after the match to arrange her parents' funeral.

"Six months later," she said, speaking to Judd in a reflective, faraway voice, "Presley was in midsentence when he gripped his chest and, without another sound, died of a heart attack. I played a scorching match the following day. He would have expected me to."

Neither her parents nor her mentor had lived to see her become the top-seeded woman player in professional tennis. This year she was on her way to getting the Grand Slam. Then she would retire, knowing she had proved her father wrong. Tennis wasn't just a rich kid's sport. It was a demanding and jealous master, one for which she'd sacrificed a college education, romance, marriage, family—everything.

Now that she was so close to mastering it, she couldn't let anything, *anything*, stand in her way.

Becoming aware that Judd was watching her closely, she unclenched her jaw and her fists and forced a tepid smile. "What about you? Did you always aspire to become a sportswriter who uses his victims' blood for ink?"

He made a face and shivered. "God, you make me sound horrible."

"You've written some horrible things about me in your articles. Why should I spare your feelings?"

"I guess a few blows below the belt are fair." He winked at her wickedly. "Come to think of it, a few blows below the belt might even be fun."

She ignored his sexual insinuation. Thinking about the kiss they'd shared—and there was no sense in fooling herself into believing that she hadn't participated—could prove hazardous.

The safest tactic was to pretend that it hadn't happened.

Judd Mackie was a reputed lady-killer. She had been victimized by his scathing prose many times. She wasn't going to fall victim to him in another area as well.

"Just out of curiosity, Mackie, why me?" She turned toward him, crooking her knee and tucking her foot beneath her hips. "Why have you singled me out to throw poison darts at?"

"Why should you care? You've got the rest of the world's population eating out of your hand. What difference does it make to you if this burned out, bummed out sportswriter gets his kicks by taking shots at you in his tacky column?"

"It's annoying."

"Not to my readers. Ever since that first article years ago—"

"For which I demanded a retraction."

He gave her a smug smile. "I printed several paragraphs of your letter, remember? Readers loved it. I got so much play out of it, I deliberately cultivated the antagonism between us."

"Why?"

"It makes for good copy."

"What did I ever do to deserve your contempt in the first place?"

"It's not so much what you've done or haven't done. It's what you are. What you . . ."

"Well?" she prompted when he left the sentence unfinished.

"It's what you look like."

That admission stunned her into silence. Finally she said, "Which is?"

"Cute. I find it very hard to take you seriously as an athlete when you look like a Barbie doll wearing a tennis dress."

"That's chauvinistic!"

"Unabashedly."

"How I look is totally irrelevant to how I play."

"Probably, but that's a chauvinistic pig for you," he quipped with an unapologetic grin.

"And if I had a wart on the end of my nose, would that make me a better tennis player in your estimation?"

"We'll never know, will we? But probably. At least I'd be less inclined to write snide things about you."

Leaning against the car door, she gazed at him with patent dismay. "For all these years I've wondered what I did to incur your wrath. And it really has nothing to do with me at all. What it boils down to is your own reverse snobbery and sexist prejudice.''

"That's a broad generalization . . . forgive me for saying no pun intended. I'm not prejudiced against women athletes at all.''

"Just me. Is there anything I can do to change your mind?''

"You could get ugly.''

"Or get cancer.''

Taking an off ramp, he came to an abrupt halt at the stop sign. Turning his head toward her, he said, "That's another of those blows beneath the belt, Stevie. But I'll overlook it on one condition.''

"What?''

"Tell me you can cook.''

"Cook?''

"Cook. You know, in a kitchen on a stove. Putting food products into pots and pans and making them edible.''

"I can cook.''

"Good,'' he replied, slipping the car into first gear and turning onto the intersecting, two-lane highway. "But nothing with a sauce. I don't like sauces, except for cream gravy on chicken-fried steak. Sauces are for sissies.''

"Oh, please," she groaned. But she was smiling.

At the next crossroad, he pulled up in front of a combination grocery store and filling station. "Let's go shopping."

A half hour later, he pulled the car onto a narrow country road. The trees growing on either side of it formed a dense green canopy overhead. The hardwoods were intermingled with tall, straight pines.

"Where in the world are we going?"

The town where they'd made their purchases hardly deserved that designation. Besides the grocery store-filling station, it had only a feed and hardware store, a post office, a fire station, a Dairy Queen, a school and three Protestant churches.

"To my grandparents' house." He laughed at the astonishment she registered. "That's right. Not only do I have a mother, but I have a father. Or did. This farm belonged to his parents. They willed it to him. When he died a few years ago, the property was handed down to me. I sold off the pastureland, but kept the twenty acres surrounding the house.''

"Twenty very beautiful acres," she noted.

"Thanks."

The house was another surprise. It was situated in a clearing surrounded by massive pecan trees that were just coming into full leaf. There was a windmill, a detached garage and a barn. All were painted white and trimmed in green. All could have used a facelift. The flower beds bordering the porch were overgrown with weeds. There was an air of desolation and neglect about the place.

"It needs some work," he remarked, understating the obvious. "It looks better on the inside, I promise."

"It's charming," Stevie said graciously. She alighted from the car, then had to duck under a spider web that had been spun from one tree to another.

Judd unlocked the front door with a key he took from beneath the welcome mat and ushered her inside. They were greeted by the dim, hushed, musty atmosphere of a house left vacant for a long time.

Standing in the wide hallway, his voice slightly echoing, he said, "Initially this was meant to be a weekend getaway, but I can rarely leave town on the weekends because so many sporting events are going on. And it's just not practical to come during the middle of the week. As a result, I don't get over here as often as I'd like or as often as the place deserves."

"What's that?" Stevie asked, nodding at the room behind him.

He pivoted on his heels. "That's a dining room with one card table, one folding chair and one portable typewriter in it." She gave him an inquiring look. "The dining-room furniture is now at my mother's house."

"Oh." That wasn't the question Stevie had in mind, but she let his explanation pass for the time being. Apparently he had done some writing here. "Upstairs?"

"Three bedrooms, one bathroom. There's also a powder room tucked behind the staircase if you're feeling the urge. No?" he said when she shook her head. "Then let's get these things into the kitchen."

She followed him past a spacious living room. All the furniture was covered with dust cloths.

They took a right turn at the end of the central hallway and entered the kitchen. Judd set the sacks of groceries on the round oak table.

"This looks like a grandma's house," Stevie commented wistfully as she ran her hand over the carved back of one of the dining chairs. "I never got to know either set of my grandparents. They died before I could really remember them."

"Whew!" Judd was at the refrigerator, lifting out something that was curled and black and, as a result, unidentifiable. He carried the foul-smelling thing at arm's length to the back door and threw it out. "Glad Grandma isn't here to see that. She'd have a fit."

He opened the windows to let in fresh air while Stevie built them sandwiches out of the cold cuts and cheeses they had bought. As she was doing it, she felt one of the twinges in her lower abdomen that she had come to recognize, almost anticipate. Strange, though, she hadn't thought much about her illness since leaving Dallas. She guessed she had Judd Mackie to thank for diverting her mind.

Only two days ago, she would have thought that if she were left alone with the columnist for any length of time, she would slowly strangle him and derive a great deal of pleasure from watching his eyeballs bulgeout of his skull as she did.

It was surprising that she found his droll sense of humor so comforting. He didn't mollycoddle or pity her, which she would have found untenable. He didn't play the clown, forcing laughter when it would have been inappropriate.

She would never have guessed that getting along with him would be so effortless. He was being the friend she needed right now, entertaining, but easy to talk to. She was glad he had come along when she needed someone who was detached, objective and uncomplicated. But she would rather have her tongue cut out than tell him so.

"Lunch is ready."

He washed his hands, then joined her at the table. "Hey, this looks great," he said enthusiastically as he straddled the seat of his chair.

Stevie took a bite of her sandwich. Through the mouthful, she asked, "What are we going to do after lunch?"

And through his mouthful of sandwich, he replied, "Make love."

Five

Stevie swallowed her bite whole and gaped at Judd who calmly swallowed and blotted his mouth with a paper napkin. "Just a suggestion, of course," he said.

In a flash, she was out of her chair and headed for the door. "I should have known better than to trust you, you... Oh! When I think how gullible I was to believe that you—Ouch!" As she sailed past his chair, he had reached out and grabbed the swishing end of her braid. Using it, he reeled her in. "Stop that!" she cried. "Let me go."

"Sit down." He tried to sound stern, but she saw that he was having difficulty keeping a straight face. "Can't you take a joke?"

"That was a joke?"

"Sure, what did you think? That I was serious?"

"Of course not!" she snapped.

"Well, then, why didn't you just laugh?"

"It wasn't funny."

"I thought so. But not near as funny as the expression on your face." He mimicked it, and if she had looked anywhere near that idiotic, she wanted to vaporize. "Kind of like you'd been hit in the face with—"

"I get the picture," she interrupted crossly as she sat down and took a savage bite out of her sandwich. "It would have been in perfect character for you to lure me here under false pretenses, then try to seduce me."

Rather than being insulted, he seemed flattered. "How do you know it would have been in character for me to seduce you?"

"I said *try* to seduce me."

"Okay. How do you know it would have been in character for me to try to seduce you?"

"One hears things," she said snootily.

"Oh, really? Like what? What have you heard about me?"

"Never mind."

"You're not referring to that story going around about me and the redheaded triplets, are you? Listen, that was a damn lie."

"Triplets?" she repeated thinly.

"They might be the most outstanding contortionists in the world, but even so..."

She eyed him suspiciously. "Are you putting me on?"

"Yeah, I'm putting you on." He resumed eating, but his smile remained insufferably complacent and amused. "Well, we know that Grandma's beds are safe from us, don't we?"

"We certainly do."

"I mean, when we kissed, nothing happened, right?"

"R-right."

"The earth didn't tremble, stars didn't pop out, fireworks didn't explode. I didn't feel much, did you?"

"No."

"No surge of lust."

"Definitely not."

He shrugged eloquently. "We tried it out and found it lacking, so you've got nothing to worry about. Now, back to your original question about what we're going to do this afternoon."

Stevie barely listened. She had been relieved to know that he was teasing about an afternoon of lovemaking, but her ego was stung. Why had he found the possibility so absurd? When they kissed, hadn't he felt even slightly feverish? Lust was a strong word to describe the tingles she'd felt in all her erogenous zones when his tongue had softly engaged hers in a mating rite, but at least she'd tingled.

He'd come away from the kiss totally unaffected. Was kissing her so unexciting that even a renowned and seemingly indiscriminate womanizer like him could come through it without feeling *something*?

"... you don't have to."

"Don't have to what?" she asked, realizing that he'd been talking all this time.

"Don't have to help," he said, looking at her strangely. "Haven't you been listening?"

"No. My mind was on something else."

His brows frowned steeply. "You're not in pain, are you?"

"No, nothing like that."

"Good." He studied her for a moment as though he wasn't convinced that she was telling the truth. When he was satisfied, he summarized what he'd been saying earlier. "I've got some chores to do around here. While I'm at it, you can relax in one of the bedrooms upstairs."

"I'd rather be outdoors. The woods are so pretty."

"Suit yourself," he said, getting up out of his chair and carrying his empty plate to the sink. "There are books on the living-room shelves. Feel free to browse if you get bored."

"Thanks."

"I brought along some work clothes. As soon as I change, I'm going to start working outside. Holler if you need anything."

"I will."

He left the kitchen. Feeling slightly dejected and deserted, Stevie turned toward the sink.

"Oh, Stevie?"

"Yes?" she said, coming around quickly.

He was peering around the edge of the door, only his head visible. "I felt a *little* surge of lust." Then, lightly slapping the doorjamb and giving her a quick wink, he vanished.

Stevie muttered foul imprecations to the empty spot where his grinning face had been.

* * *

"What the hell are you doing?"

Stevie, sitting back on her heels in the dirt, glanced over her shoulder. She almost did a double take, but caught herself just in time.

Judd was looming above her wearing nothing but a pair of dirty Levi's and a frown. In the couple of hours since she had seen him, he'd worked up a sweat. Little rivers of perspiration trickled through his plentiful chest hair. He was using a rake as a prop, one elbow resting atop the handle, his hip thrown off center.

She could see straight up into his armpit, but it seemed an invasion of his privacy to stare at that as much as it did to visually track the beads of sweat sliding down the center of his belly into the low waistband of his jeans.

Something sweet and elemental pierced through Stevie's femininity, reminding her of the twinges of pain she had been experiencing recently. But these were different. These twinges brought pleasure, not dread and doubt. But like the others, she pushed conscious thoughts of them aside because they left her feeling ambivalent and afraid.

"What does it look like I'm doing? I'm weeding this flower bed." She turned back to the task that had hopelessly soiled her white culottes and caked her hands with fertile loam. She was sweaty. Her braid was lying heavily on her damp shirt, which was clinging to her back.

She felt wonderful. It was as though this sweat was healthier than that which she worked up on the tennis court.

"You're supposed to be relaxing," Judd told her.

"This is relaxing. I enjoy tending to plants and these have been so badly neglected." She turned her head to give him a reproving look, but quickly glanced away. He was crouching behind her. Up close, his face was grimy, streaked with sweat, and more handsome than ever. She could smell his skin and knew that his lips would taste salty if he chose to kiss her just then.

Swallowing hard, she said, "There's a pitcher of ice water on the porch."

"Thanks." He eased up, groaning slightly when his knees popped, and moved up the steps to the porch. "These old bones needed the exercise, but I probably won't be able to get out of bed in the morning." He poured himself a glass of ice water. After he'd drained it, he asked, "Did you do something up here?"

"I swept. The porch was littered with leaves and pine needles. It was a disgrace."

"A regular little busy bee, aren't you?"

"It feels good to be doing honest-to-goodness work. Besides, staying busy keeps my mind occupied."

He loped down the steps and gave her long braid a playful yank. "Just don't wear yourself out."

"I won't."

"You look worn out."

The sun had already slipped behind the tops of the trees, which in turn cast slanted shadows across the clearing in front of the house. Stevie was sprawled in a bench swing suspended from the branch of a mighty pecan tree. She was idly pushing the swing with her bare foot.

Before she'd sat down in it, she'd hosed it off and swept cobwebs off the chains. They needed oil, but she rather liked the pleasant squeaking sound they made as they rocked forward and back. They were in harmony with the perpetual creaking of the windmill.

The swing had been just one of the many projects she had assigned herself during the course of the afternoon while Judd nailed up dislocated shutters, used a weed sling on the clearing, and did some major cleanup around the barn and garage.

Now, as he spoke his semichastening statement, he dropped onto the ground in front of the swing and lay on his back in the recently mowed grass.

He had put his shirt back on but left it unbuttoned. It fell open, baring his impressive chest and tantalizing stomach, which for all his carousing was flat and taut and lightly shadowed with dark hair. Stevie kept her eyes studiously averted, but it wasn't easy. It hadn't been easy to keep her eyes off him all afternoon.

"I am tired," she conceded, "but deliciously so. I don't remember when I've watched the sun sinking behind leafy trees. The dappled light, the shadows, the shades of gold and green. It's all beautiful. And the sounds—rustling forest sounds that you never hear in the city. Yet it's quiet."

He rolled to his side and rested his cheek in his palm as he gazed up at her. "Do you always rhapsodize?"

"Only when I get this tired," she said with a smile, which he returned. "I enjoyed today. It's a shame we have to go back and inhale carbon monoxide and diesel exhaust instead of resin and wildflowers."

"Do we?"

She braked the swing with her heel and lifted her head off the thick chain, on which it had been resting. "Do we what?"

"Do we have to go back?"

Her eyes narrowed on him. "What are you up to now, Mackie?"

"God, you have a suspicious nature."

"I'm not suspicious. It's just that I don't trust you as far as I can throw you," she said sweetly. "Now what do you mean by asking if we have to go back to Dallas? Of course we do."

"Why?"

"Obligations."

"To whom?"

"Well, for one, you've got an obligation to the *Tribune*."

"Not as of this morning."

"What do you mean?"

"I got fired."

She looked at him with amazement. "Fired? They *fired* you?"

"Yep."

"Why?"

"Because I let our rival newspaper scoop me on the Stevie Corbett story."

Her lips parted in surprise. For several moments she only stared at him, but could find nothing in his open expression to indicate that he was lying. She had hoped he was.

"You got fired on account of me?"

He made a negligent answer. "Don't worry about it. Firing me is one of the few things my boss enjoys. I wouldn't think of going straight and depriving him of that occasional pleasure."

His joking didn't make her smile. "But...but you could have written a dilly of a story. You're the only one who knew the truth."

"That would have made me a real son of a bitch, wouldn't it? You might find this hard to believe, but I do have some ethics, and when I say a conversation is off-the-record, it's off-the-record."

He came to his feet and moved toward the swing. Stevie was sitting at an angle, one of her legs stretched along the length of the swing. He encircled her ankle with a firm grip and lifted her leg, then sat down in the swing and laid her leg across his lap.

"You've got a blister on your foot," he observed.

"That's what I get for wearing sandals instead of tennis shoes and socks."

He rubbed the raised, red skin with the pad of his thumb. Stevie's initial plan was to pull her foot away from his massaging hand, but she reconsidered. She was afraid to move it for fear that when she did, her heel would come in contact with the bulge behind the frayed fly of his jeans. Better safe than sorry, although she wouldn't call having her foot anywhere near *that* very safe.

"We'd better get going before it gets dark," she suggested huskily.

"I meant what I said." He turned his head and speared her with his eyes. "Let's stay."

"We can't."

She wished he'd remove his hand from around her foot. He was drawing patterns in her high arch with his thumb. It was difficult not to squirm and almost impossible to keep from purring with pleasure, especially when the look he was giving her was so disarming.

"How come?"

How come? She couldn't think of a single reason. "Because."

"Good reason." He flashed her a grin, but instantly reverted to seriousness. "You need time alone to think, Stevie. What better place than here? There's no telephone, no distractions, no snoopy reporters. No one to pressure you. Just me."

Little did he know that he was the main deterrent. But because the idea held such appeal, she hedged from giving him a definite no. "You're going to sit and watch me think through my dilemma? Is that what you're proposing?"

"No, I'm going to work on my novel."

"Novel? What novel?"

"The one I'm going to start tomorrow morning. If we stay, that is. If we don't, the great American novel will never be written and everybody'll be blaming you."

"Oh, thanks. So now your career is my responsibility."

"Well, I *did* get fired because of you," he reminded her gently.

"You just said—"

"I know what I said," he said grumpily. "Look, let's stay. You can putter in the flower bed and around the house, cook and clean, and I'll write."

"Free maid service, that's what you want." She pulled her foot from his warm grasp, hoping for the best. Her heel grazed the button fly on his jeans, but she didn't let her mind dwell on the solid fullness she felt beneath it. "You want a housekeeper at your beck and call while you're playing John Steinbeck. You're a con, Mackie, a big con. The most manipulative—"

"You can lie in bed the livelong day for all I care," he said loudly, overriding her protests. "*You* are the one who said you wanted to stay busy to keep your mind off..." His eyes skittered down toward her lap. "You know."

Then he lifted his eyes to hers. One look into her hostile gaze and he blew out a disgusted breath. "Okay, forget I mentioned it. Bad idea. I thought both of us could use some time away from the grind to think, reassess, plan, that kind of thing. This seemed the perfect place for it. Obviously I was wrong on all accounts.''

He left the swing. It rocked crazily. Stevie steadied it with her foot. ''Where would we sleep?'' she asked his retreating back.

He came to an abrupt halt and for several seconds didn't move. When he did, he came around slowly. '' 'Where would *we* sleep'?''

''Where would *I* sleep?''

''You get first pick of the bedrooms.''

''Where would you sleep?''

''In one of the other bedrooms.'' He propped his hands on his hips. ''Is *that* what you're thinking, that I have an ulterior motive? A combined housekeeper and mistress.'' She remained stonily silent and accusatory. ''I thought we'd already established that there's no sexual chemistry between us,'' he said. ''Look, I meant this to be a purely platonic setup. Right now both our lives are in upheaval. Why would we want any additional complications?''

''Exactly.''

''I don't see any sparks arcing between us, do you?''

''No.''

"Would you go around all dirty and sweaty and generally looking like hell if you were trying to tempt me into being your lover?"

"No," Stevie said stiffly, wanting very badly to slap him.

"So fine. Neither would I. If I wanted you in my bed, I'd come right out and say so. Geez," he breathed, raking his fingers through his hair. "Now that that's understood, do we go or stay?"

Six

○~⌒~⌒~○

"I thought it would be nice to eat out here."

Stevie gestured awkwardly at the card table she had brought from the dining room onto the front porch. She'd gathered a colorful bouquet of wildflowers and placed it in the center of the table. A raid of closets and cupboards had produced a tablecloth, linen napkins, even a candle, which, with the help of melted wax, she'd managed to stand in a saucer. The light flickered onto Judd's shadowed face.

"Great idea, but you went to too much trouble."

"I enjoyed it."

As promised, he had given her first pick of the bedrooms. She had chosen the one facing east because she was accustomed to waking up early.

Her choice pleased him because he admitted that the last thing he wanted to see in the morning was sunlight pouring through the shutters.

Moving from the bedroom, he had showed her into the bathroom. It had a pedestal sink and an old-fashioned claw-footed tub.

"At least seven feet long and suitable for re-clining if you're in the mood for a long soak," he had said with the nasal accent of a snake-oil vendor.

They had found towels and sheets, along with a few odds and ends of clothing, in the upstairs linen closet. Judd had looked skeptically at the clothes. "Think you can find something to wear until we get into town?"

"I'll manage. Who did these clothes belong to?" she asked, holding a full skirt up against her.

"Assorted cousins I guess." There was a mix of men's and women's apparel. Judd took a shirt and pair of shorts. "Just because I'm such a nice guy, I'll let you go first in the bathroom. If it's okay with you, we'll cook those steaks I bought today for dinner." Her stomach had rumbled as though on cue. He made a scrubbing motion against it with his knuckles. "Guess that means you approve."

Stevie had tightened her stomach muscles in defense against his touch and tried to pretend that she still had sufficient breath. But for all her efforts, her voice still sounded unnaturally soprano when she said, "Steak sounds wonderful."

"Okay, I'll go start the charcoal while you're bathing. I found granddad's grill in the garage and scrubbed it clean today. There was even a sack of charcoal."

A half hour later, she had met him coming up as she was returning downstairs. She was fresh and clean, her hair still damp. He was dirtier than ever. Besides the grime he'd collected during the day, he'd added an overall dusting of charcoal powder.

"The water comes out rusty," she had told him. "But if you let it run a second or two it clears up."

"Thanks for the warning," he had replied as he trudged past her.

Now, they faced each other over the candlelit table. The night sounds coming from the surrounding woods were loud and distinct, the smell of cooking steaks mouth-watering, the breeze balmy.

Stevie, feeling foolishly nervous and self-conscious, groped for something to say. "The coals were just right."

"Good."

"I went ahead and put the steaks on the grill, but you might want to check them."

She was plagued by a sudden shyness and couldn't imagine where it had originated. Maybe the peasant blouse had been a poor choice; it was making her feel foolishly feminine. It was a size too large. The neckline was wide and kept slipping off one shoulder. If her clothes hadn't been so dirty, she would have put them back on after her bath.

As it was, she was standing before a man who could joke about bedding triplet contortionists, feeling ridiculously gauche and vulnerable.

He surveyed it all: the candle, the flowers, the table setting, her. Especially her. He left his eyes on her for a long, ponderously quiet moment. "Trying to impress me, Stevie? Maybe I should warn you before your heart gets broken that I'm not the marrying kind."

The sensual bubble burst. "You conceited jerk!" she cried indignantly, planting her hands on her hips. "I didn't do this for you. I did it for me. I rarely get to entertain and when I do, I usually take my guests out to dinner. This was a rare—What are you laughing at?"

"You. You can't take a joke worth a damn, but you're cuter than ever when you get riled."

Stevie stood there stewing while he moved to the grill, which he'd set up in one corner of the porch. She vacillated over whether or not to finish giving him a piece of her mind, but decided to leave well enough alone. Invariably their verbal skirmishes came out in his favor.

Over his shoulder, he said, "Five more minutes and the steaks will be perfect."

Stevie used that five minutes to carry out the green salad she had made, a loaf of French bread she had buttered and left warming in the oven and a pitcher of iced tea she had garnished with fresh mint she had discovered growing on either side of the back porch.

Judd sipped from his tall, icy glass and smacked his lips with appreciation. "The mint in the tea really reminds me of summers I spent here on the farm with my grandparents." For a moment he stared reflectively into space.

"What?" Stevie asked softly.

He focused on her and snorted a self-derisive laugh. "I just realized that happy hour has come and gone and I hadn't even missed it." He saluted her with his glass of tea. "Must be your company."

She basked in the warm glow coming from his eyes and began eating. A few moments later she said, "The steak is delicious, Judd."

"Well, don't get too excited. This about exhausts my culinary talents."

They resumed eating in silence. To make conversation, Stevie asked, "What's your novel about?"

"Writers never talk about the pieces they're currently working on."

"You haven't started working on it yet."

"Same rules apply to an idea."

"Why don't you talk about it?"

"Because talking about the story dilutes the compulsion to write it down."

"Oh." She returned to her food, but her mind stayed on that track. "I can understand that, I think. Before an important match, I don't like to talk about it. I don't want to discuss my strategy or the odds either against or in my favor. I'm immersed in my own thoughts. Sharing them would jinx the match.''

"You're superstitious," he accused, pointing the tines of his fork at her.

"I didn't think so until now. But maybe so." She finished her food and pushed the plate aside. "I take my game very seriously. That's why your column has always been such a bone of contention, Mr. Mackie. You poke fun at me."

"It sells newspapers. I realize you take your game seriously. Maybe you take it too seriously."

"There's no such thing."

"Isn't there?" he asked, propping his elbows on the table and leaning closer to the burning candle. The flame flickered across his features, softening them, but enhancing their masculinity. "Where's the husband, the kids, the house?"

"If I were a man would you be asking me those questions?"

"Probably not," he admitted. "But then..." His eyes lowered to the neckline of the white peasant blouse. "You're not a man."

While she'd been busy eating, she had forgotten to give her neckline an upward tug every so often. It had dipped to cleavage level. The shadows cast by the single wavering candle made the valley between her breasts look velvety and mysterious.

Stevie, feeling threatened by his hot gaze and the personal slant their conversation had taken, immediately threw up a defensive wall and went back to their generic topic. "Everything, even success, comes with a price tag attached. You can't have it all."

"Some do. But not you. You don't have anything but your game."

"A damned good game," she said testily.

"Granted. But I bet if you polled most sportswriters, *male* sportswriters, and asked them what Stevie Corbett's finest contribution to tennis is, they wouldn't say, 'Her backhand.' If they were being honest, they'd more than likely say, 'Her backside.' It's just that I've got the guts to say, or write, what the rest of them are thinking."

She scooted back her chair and stood up quickly. "You're incorrigible, Mackie."

"So I've been told by everybody from my nursery-school teacher to Mike Ramsey as recently as this morning. He said—Stevie?'' Judd slid out of his chair and rounded the corners of the table in one motion. ''What's the matter?''

''Nothing.''

''Dammit,'' he swore, ''don't tell me nothing. Are you in pain?''

She took several swift, shallow breaths. ''Sometimes, whenever I move too suddenly, like just then, it hurts a little.''

Judd pressed his hand against her lower abdomen. ''Do you need your pain pills? Sit down, goddammit. I'll go get them.''

''No, it's fine. Much better.'' When she glanced up at him, her smile was tentative, but brave. ''It leaves as fast as it comes. I'm alright now.''

His fingers pressed into her abdomen, kneading her through the skirt. ''You sure?''

She was sure of only one thing, and that was that if he didn't take his hand away and stop doing with it what he was doing, her desire-weakened knees were going to buckle and her mouth would reach for a taste of his.

''I'm sure,'' she replied thickly.

He searched her eyes, seemingly reluctant to believe her, but several heartbeats later, he withdrew his hand and stepped away. "You'd better go upstairs and lie down."

"Nonsense. It was just a twinge."

"Twinges don't make your lips go white."

"Kindly step aside so I can start clearing the table."

"Hell, no. Leave the dishes until tomorrow morning."

"I wouldn't think of it. Your grandmother would never forgive me. Now move."

He did so, but grudgingly, while he muttered curses beneath his breath. "How often do these twinges strike you?" he asked as he followed her into the house, bearing a tray of dirty dishes.

"Maybe once, twice a day. Really they're nothing to worry about." She filled the sink with soapy water. Each time she tried to move in any direction, she nearly stepped on him. "You're underfoot, Mackie. Why don't you be a good boy and go outside and play? Or work on your novel."

He slammed out of the kitchen, mumbling beneath his breath as he went through the shadowed rooms of the house. He knew pain when he saw it, and Stevie had been in pain. Did she think he was stupid enough to fall for her glib dismissal of it?

"A 'twinge,' my ass," he thought out loud.

She had downplayed that reminder of her illness the way he was currently de-emphasizing the swelling behind his fly. He wouldn't dare call it what it was. But what else could it be?

Stevie Corbett had been the warmest, softest thing he'd ever touched. Removing his hand from the folds of her skirt had been the hardest thing he'd ever had to do. He didn't know how he'd kept from touching her breasts just to see if they felt as fantastic as they looked.

To take his mind off how good she smelled and how badly he wanted to kiss her again and how much he ached, he carried the card table back into the dining room and set it up.

He positioned the lamp just so, adjusting the cheap lamp shade for maximum light. He replaced the typewriter and the ream of paper, stacking it and restacking it until all the edges were as straight as a knife blade. He checked the typewriter ribbon and made certain that pencils and erasers were within reach.

Then he just stood there, staring down at the card table, flexing his fingers at his sides.

"What are you doing?"

He spun around. Stevie was watching him curiously from the arched doorway.

"I'm setting up," he answered cantankerously. "You don't just jump into writing without setting up, you know. It takes lots of preparation."

"Oh. It looked like you were just standing there, shivering in your shoes, knees knocking, afraid to start."

"Well I wasn't."

"Okay, okay." She took a step backward as though she had roused an ill-tempered wild beast, which wasn't too far from the truth. "I'm going into the living room to read."

"Fine. Don't make any racket, will ya?"

"I won't."

"Say, wait!" He went after her when she turned away. "I didn't mean to snap at you like that. This is our first night here. The country is making me jittery, I guess."

"No city noise."

"Something like that. I've got it!" He snapped his fingers. "Want to play cards? I'm sure I can find a deck around here somewhere."

"I'm tired, Judd. Maybe another night."

"Trivia? We'll make up our own questions. You can choose the categories."

"I'd rather just read."

"Okay. That's fine. I'll help you select a book."

But as he went past her, she grabbed his arm and hauled him back. "I'll find my own book. Quit stalling, Mackie."

"Stalling?"

"Stalling. You're stalling like a kid at bedtime. That novel isn't going to write itself."

"Is that what you think I'm doing? Stalling to keep from starting on my book?"

"Yes."

"Geez, no wonder you never got married," he grumbled, as he turned back toward the dining room. "Who would want to marry you? You're no fun. No fun at all."

Stevie caught herself nodding off. She finally admitted defeat and laid her book on the end table. Earlier that day she'd uncovered all the furniture in the living room. It was basic Early American, constructed largely of maple, nothing she would have decorated with herself, but in perfect keeping with the rest of the house.

She switched off the lamp and retrieved her sandals from the floor, carrying them as she crossed the wide hallway. Judd was prowling the dining room, rolling his head around his shoulders and flexing the muscles of his arms. There were several models of paper airplanes scattered about the floor. One had crashed into the drapery cornice.

"How's it coming?" She moved toward the table, glanced down at the paper in the typewriter and read what he'd written so far. "'Chapter One.' Very insightful."

"Very cute."

"You're a long way from a Pulitzer, Mackie."

"And you're a long way from a Grand Slam."

His words extinguished the teasing light in her eyes and caused her smile to collapse. "You're right. I am."

He swore liberally as he plowed all his fingers through his hair. "I'm sorry. I didn't mean . . . I didn't think . . . I wasn't referring to—"

"I knew what you meant. No harm done. What's the matter with your shoulders?"

"Nothing."

"You're wincing every time you move."

"Too much of the weed sling, I guess."

"Really?" Pulling a worried face, she moved toward him and dropped her sandals onto the floor. She lifted her hands to his shoulders and squeezed the muscles lightly.

He yelped. "Ouch, damn, they hurt enough without you digging into them like that."

"You're as cranky as an old bear."

"Yeah? Well that's what I feel like. The first morning after hibernation."

"Come on upstairs. I'll give you a rubdown with this stuff that I'm never without."

She picked up her sandals again; he turned out the lamp. Together they started upstairs. "What kind of stuff?" he asked warily.

"A lotion. A sports injury specialist developed it. It's guaranteed to get rid of all stiffness and swelling."

She was several steps ahead of him. He caught the hem of her skirt and pulled her up short. She turned inquisitively.

"If it's guaranteed to do that," he drawled, "you gotta promise not to rub it on any parts I haven't okayed first."

Seven

Snatching her skirt out of his hand, Stevie shot him a quelling look and continued upstairs. After getting the bottle of lotion from the tote bag she'd brought along, she went to his bedroom door. "Knock, knock."

"Come in."

She did...just as he was peeling off his T-shirt. With his arms stretched high over his head, standing beneath the overhead light fixture, he was granting Stevie an unrestricted view of his body: the broad shoulders, wide chest, trim torso, narrow hips, scarred leg.

Scarred leg?

The T-shirt cleared his head. As he lowered his arms, he caught her staring at the jagged, purple scars that crisscrossed his left shin. He balled the

T-shirt into a wad and, with a hook shot, tossed it into the easy chair near the bed.

"It's not polite to stare."

The chip on his shoulder had doubled in size since she'd entered the room. She could hear the insolence in his voice, an overcompensating sarcasm. Maybe she had accidentally happened upon Judd Mackie's one spot of vulnerability.

It would be ludicrous to pretend she hadn't seen the scars. Even if she could pull off such an act, he wouldn't fall for it and would resent her attempt. Her curiosity wasn't morbid, but sympathetic. There was no better way to deal with the awkward situation than to be straightforward.

"What happened to your leg, Judd?"

"Compound fracture of the tibia."

Worse than she had thought. She didn't even try to hide her grimace. "How?"

"Waterskiing accident."

"When?"

"A long time ago," he answered with a mix of bitterness and sadness. He moved toward her. She followed the progress of the scarred limb, lowering her eyes as he came closer in order to keep it in view. Judd placed his finger beneath her chin and tilted it up. "If you keep gawking, you're going to give me a complex."

"I'm sorry," she said, meaning it. "It's just that you've been wearing shorts all night and I didn't notice the scars until just now." It had been dark on the porch and his legs had been beneath the table while they ate. The angles hadn't been right at any other time. "It came as a shock, that's all. I wasn't prepared, didn't expect it."

"Most women find that leg incredibly sexy."

Now that she'd seen it, been stunned by it, he wanted to tease her shock away. That was fine with her. She would play along for now and ruminate later on the injury that had healed, but which remained a supersensitive spot to the seemingly invincible sportswriter.

"Oh, it's sexy alright," she told him with an impish grin. "Devilishly so. Almost as good as the hairy chest."

"No lie?"

"No lie. My mouth's watering."

"Hmm."

He lowered his eyes to her lips. His intense gaze was as stirring and provocative as his scathing prose, though in an entirely different way. The bottom seemed to drop out of Stevie's stomach. Before she became hopelessly trapped by his stare, which seemed to be drawing her closer to him like a powerful magnet, she turned away from him and began vigorously shaking the bottle of lotion.

"Where do you want to do this?"

"I don't know," he answered in a low voice. "How well are we going to get to know each other?"

She spun around to find him standing very close behind her, looking hungrily at her exposed neck while he played with the end of her braid. As he rubbed the silky strands between his fingers, he whispered, "There's the chair. Or there's the bed."

She flicked his hand away. "Do you want a rubdown or not?"

"I do."

"Then sit down and let's get it over with."

"I guess that means the chair," he said dryly, making an effort to keep from smiling. He pulled a straight chair from beneath a desk and straddled the seat, folding his arms over the back of it. "Have at me."

Stevie moved to stand behind him. She filled one palm with the lotion, then rubbed it against the other. However, when it came time to actually touch him, she hesitated. He had his chin propped on his stacked hands. Eventually her hesitation brought his head around.

"What's the matter?"

"Nothing."

"This isn't going to burn or anything, is it?"

"Chicken?"

"When it comes to my hide, you bet your ass."

"Do you think I'd smear it on my own hands if it burned?" she asked crossly.

"I don't know. You might. I've written some rotten things about you. This might be your way of getting revenge."

"Which you sorely deserve."

The conversation had given her time to bolster her courage. She laid her hands on his naked shoulders and began massaging in the healing lotion.

"Hmm," he moaned pleasurably after several moments. "Not bad, Stevie."

"Thanks. I've had lots of practice."

"On whom?"

"Other players on the tour."

"Men?"

"Sometimes."

"Oh, yeah? Is there material for a column here? 'Locker Room Lechery'?"

"That sounds like you. Low, mean, base."

"'Tennis Court Courtship'?"

"Ghastly headline."

"'Racquets and Romance'? 'Overhands, Or Head Over Heels?'?"

The freckles that dotted the ridge of his shoulders were adorable. They begged to have kisses pecked on them. The skin beneath Stevie's slippery fingers was taut, the muscles supple.

She wanted to slide her hands down his sides and over the corrugated rib cage. The fuzziness in his armpits intrigued her. With her eyes, she followed his spine into the waistband of his shorts. Touching him hadn't satisfied a building curiosity. It had only heightened it.

"Well, how 'bout it?" His mouth was pressed against his hands so the words came out mumbled. Her massage was lulling him. His eyes were closed. For such a tough guy, his eyelashes were ridiculously thick.

"How about what?"

"Romance. Ever had to use your racquet to beat off the circuit Romeos?"

"Never."

"Not your style, huh?"

"What is my style?" she asked.

"To give an unwanted suitor one of those cool, condescending stares of yours. That would chill most men to the bone."

"So far it hasn't worked on you, Mackie."

"As you said, I'm incorrigible. If I'd taken every woman's first no as final, I'd still be a virgin." He sighed. "Keep this up, Stevie, and you can have your way with me."

"Don't play so hard to get."

Even though he didn't open his eyes, they crinkled at the corners when he smiled. His eyebrows were as dense as his lashes. They were the eyebrows of a man with integrity, although integrity was a term she would never have applied to Judd Mackie. Not until yesterday, when, out of respect for her dilemma, he had let another sportswriter scoop him on a big story.

That unselfish decision had gotten him fired from the *Tribune*. Didn't that indicate that under that tough, bad-boy veneer, there was a man of honor?

"Do my arms, too."

"My fingers are getting tired," she complained. "This massage business is hard work."

"Just do it."

Her complaint had been a token one. She was deriving as much pleasure from the massage as he. His biceps were as firm as green apples and as finely shaped. She squeezed them hard, watching the deep impressions her fingers made in his flesh. When she let go, white stripes were left on the tanned skin. He grunted with animal pleasure.

"You accused me of missing my calling," he said. "I think I just figured out what you should have been."

Stevie realized then that Judd wasn't the only one being stimulated by the massage. She had moved closer to him, until her middle was lightly grinding against his back with each motion of her hands.

Realizing that, she suddenly withdrew them. "That's all I can do," she said, silently adding, "Without making a fool of myself."

Reluctantly he raised his head and pivoted his bottom until he was sitting correctly in the chair. He spread his knees wide, placed his hands around her waist and drew her between his legs.

"Mackie?" she said breathlessly.

"Hmm?"

"What are we doing?"

"Doing? Nothing."

He laid his hand on her abdomen again, with his fingers pointed up toward her breasts. "Any more pain?" He applied pressure to her lower body with the heel of his hand.

Unable to speak, she shook her head no.

"Positive?" His fingers curled into the softness of her belly, then relaxed again.

"Positive."

"Good." He'd been watching the movement of his own hand. Now his eyes scaled up her body until they connected with hers. "You'd tell me, wouldn't you?"

The demand was disguised in the form of a polite question. "Yes. I'd tell you."

Keeping his gaze locked with hers, he slid his hand up the center of her body until it covered her heart, which was beating heavily.

"You smell good." He leaned forward and nuzzled her breasts, bumping them with his nose. "Where'd you find the perfume?"

"I brought my own." Stevie was barely able to form the words while his head was moving from one side of her body to the other and his hand was catching each of her drumming heartbeats.

"I like it."

"Thank you."

"You're welcome."

She whimpered when his lips touched the bare skin of her chest just above the slipping neckline of the peasant blouse. Briefly his lips brushed across her cleavage. Gradually, slowly, he kissed his way up her chest and throat as he came out of the chair.

When he was standing, feet still widespread, he encircled her waist with one arm and pulled her against him. His lips covered hers as his hand curved around her breast.

"Mackie . . . ?"

"Judd."

"Judd . . . ?"

"Go with it, Stevie."

His lips parted, so did hers. When they met again, their tongues touched and each released a low, satisfied, and conversely hungry sound. His mouth was as warmly possessive as his hand upon her breast, which he reshaped with his gently flexing fingers. Her nipple became hard and flushed beneath the idle sweeping motions of his thumb.

He dipped his head and kissed her through the blouse, leaving a damp, sheer spot on the soft cloth. Noticing that as he raised his head, he molded the wet fabric around her nipple until it clung, delineated, made visible.

His nostrils flared slightly and he muttered irreverently and arousingly. When his lips returned to hers, he kissed her with more depth and urgency and wildness.

"Stevie, don't worry, baby," he rasped against her lips, "you're more than enough woman for any man."

When the words registered, a wildfire of a different sort rampaged through Stevie's already burning body. She tore her mouth from beneath his and sent him sprawling across the hardwood floor when she pushed him away.

"So that's it!" She was seething, angrier than she'd ever been in her life, angrier than she'd ever been over a rotten line call or a lousy draw. "That's why you're being so nice to me. That's what all the sexual innuendos and pawing are about. You feel sorry for me."

"Huh?" Judd blinked his eyes back into focus. "What the hell are you talking about?"

"Your kindness and concern, your unselfish invitation to share this rural refuge with you, your flattery and sly come-ons." Clenching her teeth, she slapped her hands against the sides of her thighs. "Lord, I can't believe I was stupid enough to fall for it."

"Does this tirade have a point?"

He was looking up at her darkly, obviously none too pleased that she'd cut their party short. But his anger didn't come close to the level of hers.

"I don't need your pity, Mr. Mackie," she said heatedly.

"*Pity?* Pity didn't put this here," he said, briefly touching his fly.

"Then if your motivation isn't pity, that makes you even more despicable. You're manipulative. You figured I'd be easy to get into bed because I was panicked over losing my womanhood."

He released a series of creative curses. Aiming a finger at her, he said, "You should be the one writing the novel. You've got the imagination for it."

Stevie was pacing the width of the room. "While you were at it, you thought you would soften me up, get me to talk about every private aspect of my life. Then, when we returned to Dallas, you planned to write a really bang-up story that would ingratiate you with your boss again, sell newspapers, and leave the competitor who scooped you with egg on his face because you got the *real* story."

"I don't believe this." Still sitting on the floor, he laughed softly and shook his head.

"Let me tell you something." She stood above him, quaking with fury. "I don't need a Neanderthal like you to restore my faith in my femininity. Even if the surgeon does have to take everything out, I'll be more a woman than you are a man. A real man doesn't have to resort to the lowest, sneakiest form of trickery to get a woman into bed with him."

"That's the highest pile of crap I've come up against in a long time." He came to his feet so that they were standing toe to toe. "I'm not about to honor it with a comment, much less a denial."

"No matter what you said now, I wouldn't believe you."

"That's why I won't waste my breath."

"You're a lying con man. Your writing stinks. Your column is a joke. Being in your company makes me sick, and I've eaten much better steaks!" She tossed her braid over her shoulder and took a calming breath. "I want to leave. Right now. Drive me back to Dallas."

"Forget it."

"*Now* I said."

"*No* I said. You can stand there and fume all night if you want to, but I did the work of ten men today. I'm tired. I'm going to bed."

He unfastened the shorts. They dropped to the floor and he stepped out of them. Then he peeled off his briefs. Nonchalantly he moved toward the bed, flung back the covers, hit the wall switch of the overhead light and got into bed.

"G'night."

Stevie was sitting at the kitchen table the following morning when he came sauntering in. He was idly scratching his bare chest and yawning broadly.

"Ah, coffee, good." He took a cup out of the cabinet and filled it, then leaned against the drain board to drink the brew. "Got your bags all packed, I see."

Wearing an amused expression, he nodded toward the large canvas tote bag she'd brought with her the day before. It was propped against her chair. She was dressed in her own clothes. They were filthy, but her bearing was one of superiority.

"Sleep well?" he asked guilelessly.

"No."

"Gee, that's too bad. I slept better than I have in months, maybe years. What was your problem, bed too soft?"

She gave him her iciest stare. "I guess I should thank you for putting on some shorts before coming downstairs." That was all he had on, but more than he'd been wearing the last time she'd seen him.

"Actually I enjoy drinking my first cup of the morning in the buff, so the shorts are a real concession in your honor." He executed a quick, little bow.

"Go to hell."

He laughed. "Come on, Stevie, lighten up. If we're going to be staying here together—"

"We're not. I'm going back to Dallas. If you won't drive me, I'll take a bus."

"There is no bus."

"Then I'll hitchhike."

"I'd pay to watch that."

"I'll find a way home," she shouted.

"Are you still mad at me? Look, you know that everything you said last night is garbage. Taking pity on you and getting you here under my roof just so I could bed you while you're in a vulnerable state of mind is all hogwash."

"Is it? I don't think so."

"Believe me, baby, the only reason I ever kiss a woman is because I want to. Pity has never extended that far."

"You said yesterday that you wanted this arrangement to be platonic, that seduction wasn't what you had in mind."

"Okay, so I told a fib. It was a tiny one." She didn't return his beatific smile. He tilted his head down and peered up at her from beneath his eyebrows. "I think you're madder at yourself than you are at me."

"Why would I be mad at myself?"

His grin was egotistical and knowledgeable. "You didn't want to enjoy kissing me, but you did."

"You . . . you . . ."

"No need to get huffy. I was enjoying it, too," he said, raising his hands helplessly. "I couldn't very well hide the fact, could I?"

She quickly averted her eyes. "I don't know what you're talking about."

"The hell you don't. See, Stevie, that's what happens to a man when he caresses a woman's breast. Even kissing it through her blouse is a real turn-on." His voice lowered an octave.

"And your nipple wouldn't have been so easy to find through your blouse if you hadn't been as aroused as I was. So what are you going to do, shoot me for behaving and responding normally? If so, you're gonna have to shoot yourself, too. That's only fair."

Her cheeks were flaming. Her whole body was as hot as a furnace. All her extremities were throbbing. His words had evoked stirrings within her she wished she could forget. But after unsuccessfully battling them all night, it didn't seem likely that they would simply vanish over breakfast, especially with Judd fanning the coals of her recollection.

"I want to go home," she said sternly. "You put on a sincere dog-and-pony show yesterday, but you brought me here for self-serving reasons."

"Nope, Stevie, that's not why you're angry." He set his empty coffee cup on the countertop and moved toward her. "You're not even mad because I stripped down in front of you."

She inclined away from him, until she was at risk of falling out of her chair. "Of course that's why I'm mad."

"Then why didn't you take the car and strike out for Dallas on your own?"

"I thought of it!"

"Well?"

"It was late," she said, hoping he couldn't tell that she was grasping at straws.

In fact, she hadn't thought of leaving by herself. After seeing him naked, all she had thought about was distancing herself from him before she did something really foolish, like follow him into bed.

She'd gone to her room, got into her own bed and lain as stiff as a board, afraid to move for fear that her churning body would prompt her into committing a rash and regrettable act. For all his swaggering this morning, she might just as well have.

If he were this disgustingly arrogant when she resisted, imagine how obnoxious he would be if she ever gave in. It didn't bear thinking about.

He was waiting for a plausible answer. She said the first thing that popped into her head. "I wasn't sure I could find my way along these country roads back to the interstate."

He gave her a smug look that told her at once he knew she was lying. "Uh-huh." Bracing his arms on the table, he leaned over her. "You got upset because last night reminded you of Stockholm."

Eight

If his goal had been to knock the props out from under her, he had succeeded. She made several vain attempts to speak, opening and closing her mouth like the dummy of a ventriloquist with laryngitis. Finally she was able to croak, "I didn't think you remembered."

"I do."

"You were drunk."

"Not that drunk."

Leaving the chair, she ducked under one of his imprisoning arms. The coffeepot shook in her hand as she refilled her cup. She sipped it for fortification and to give her eyes something to look at besides the triumphant gleam in Judd's.

He thought he had her at a disadvantage. He did. The only way she was going to save face was to brazen it out. She assumed a haughty, indifferent air.

"Stockholm happened a long time ago, Mackie. Ten or eleven years, for heaven's sake. It wasn't any big deal."

"Oh, no?" He sprawled in one of the kitchen chairs, thrusting his bare feet out in front of him and crossing them at the ankles. "The shindig at that place was one of the best damn parties I've ever been to."

"You crashed it."

He chuckled. "See, that's the beauty of party crashing. You get to choose the very best ones to go to."

"You and your pals bribed—"

"Charmed."

"—your way inside. You upset—"

"Entertained."

"—everybody. The hosts were mortified—"

"—Amused."

Stevie sighed with annoyance. "I see we remember it differently."

"Admit it. My group livened things up considerably."

"That much I will admit." Her lips ached to surrender to the smile tugging at the corners of them. "Until you showed up, it was a stuffy and boring affair."

"After the hubbub we created had died down a bit, my well-trained radar system homed in on the prettiest woman there." His eyes found hers across the homey kitchen, just as they had across the ballroom of a Swedish palace so many years earlier. "You."

"Thank you. But I was also the youngest."

"I was young, too," he remarked introspectively. "I didn't realize how young. That was before I got the job at the *Tribune*. I was working for a news service, covering sports in Europe. My leg..."

He shook his head, clearing it of that unhappy thought. "I had a helluva good time over there, hanging out with all the sports celebrities, hobnobbing with royalty, going to parties, eating free food, drinking free booze."

"Picking up free women."

"The job definitely had its perks." He flashed his most unrepentant smile.

"I was so naive," she said in a reflective tone that echoed his. "That was my first year on the tour. I hadn't been warned against predatory media wolves like you."

"That was a stroke of good fortune for me."

Stevie snapped to attention and said with emphasis, "Nothing happened."

"That's not the way I remember it."

"Okay, we danced. You rudely cut in on my other partner."

"After you gave me that smoldering come-hither look."

"Smoldering? Come-hither? Boy, is your memory warped."

"And I didn't cut in, I just sort of nudged your partner out of my way. Besides, his dancing reminded me of a goose flapping its wings."

She smiled at the memory of her partner and Judd's unflattering, but accurate, description. "No, he couldn't dance very well."

But Judd could. Oh, he could. He had ignored the gyrating couples surrounding them on the dance floor and had pulled her into his arms.

Hi.

That's all he had said. That single Americanism. But there had been something totally captivating in the way he'd said it, softly, confidentially, as though they were meeting in a hushed, remote place instead of in a gigantic ballroom seething with laughter and deafening rock music.

He had mesmerized her with his compelling tone of voice and the possessive way his hands had settled on either side of her waist and pulled her swaying hips directly against his.

He had been everything she wasn't: sophisticated, cocky, self-assured, arrogant, undisciplined. He was out to enjoy life, make friends, have a good time.

She thought of little except her tennis game. Her constant companion was Presley Foster. Their conversations revolved solely around tennis and how tough the competition was and how far she had to go to get into the big bucks and the big time. She was self-disciplined to a fault. Even attending a party and staying out that late had been a rarity.

The handsome sports journalist was fascinating—and dangerous. He danced close enough for her to feel his breath on her face, held her in a manner that wasn't decorous, looked at her suggestively and moved his lithe body against hers with blatant symbolism. He had made dedicated, disciplined Stevie Corbett feel deliciously reckless.

"And after we danced, you went upstairs with me."

"You're dreaming, Mackie." Stevie wished her voice sounded stronger, more derisive. Instead it sounded hoarse and emotional. "I went into the garden and you followed."

"You ran."

"I needed air!"

"You were scared!"

She was scared. Scared of him and of her responses to him. Scared of the sensual awakening he had orchestrated. Scared because for the first time in many years, tennis was the last thing on her mind.

"I guess now you're going to ungallantly remind me that you kissed me."

Judd's steady gaze didn't waver. "You kissed me back."

She cleared her throat and made an off-handed gesture. "It was...pleasant."

"I'll say. Damned pleasant. Pleasant and wet and hot and sexy."

"Alright," she flared, "so we kissed."

"French kissed."

"French kissed."

"And I put my hand inside your dress. I touched you."

"An outrageous thing to do," she whispered.

"Was it?" He rolled off his spine and came to his feet. He didn't stop moving forward until he had her backed against the countertop. "You were soft and very sweet, Stevie. Your heart was beating so fast. Just like it was last night." He laid his hand against her chest. "Just like it is right now."

"Nothing happened."

He dropped his hand and stepped back. "Because Presley Foster bore down on me and threatened me with castration if I didn't get my hands off you."

Stevie covered her face with her hands, feeling again all the embarrassment she had at that black moment in her life. She had wanted the earth to swallow her whole, so she wouldn't have to endure her coach's censorious glare, Judd's contemptuous smirk or her own scalding humiliation.

"Presley was doing what he thought was best for me," she said miserably. "He was protecting me from getting hurt."

"Were you sleeping with him?"

She lowered her hands and gaped at Judd with horror, her face pale and stricken. "Are you crazy?"

"Were you?"

"No!" She gulped reflexively. "Is that what you've thought all this time, that I was sleeping with my coach?"

"It crossed my mind."

"You're sick."

He shook his head ruefully. "Just realistic. I've known of kinkier relationships."

"Then you've been around people I never want to meet."

"Indubitably."

Staring into space, she organized her thoughts. "Well, this conversation explains a lot. No wonder you've taken potshots at me in your column. Either you took me for a slut with a lover older than her father. Or I'm just one that got away. Either way, your phenomenal ego couldn't handle my choosing Presley over you that night, so you carved me to bits in your columns as vengeance."

"One has nothing to do with the other."

"I'll bet," she said bitterly.

He grabbed her upper arm. "It was years before I connected the champion player Stevie Corbett with that wide-eyed kid I met at a party in Stockholm."

"When you did, I bet you had a good laugh." Angrily she pulled her arm from his grip.

"Not really," he surprised her by saying. "When I think back to that night, it's with poignancy, not derision. Want to know one of my deepest, darkest secrets? Even if Foster hadn't stopped it, I doubt it would have gone much further than it had."

"Why not?"

"You were so damned young. Innocent. Fresh. And I . . . well, I wasn't."

She was almost hypnotized by the sadness in his expression. However, in the nick of time, she narrowed her eyes suspiciously and asked, "If you knew I was innocent and fresh, then why'd you just ask me if I was sleeping with Presley?"

"Oh, I knew you weren't sleeping with him then. You were a virgin in Stockholm, right?" She opened her mouth to speak, but again discovered that she was too flabbergasted to utter a peep. "But I wanted to know if you had *ever* slept with him and were still carrying a torch. Now I know you didn't and you aren't.''

Propping her hands on her hips, she glared up at him. ''You sneaky lowlife, underhanded son-ofa—''

''Before you launch into another round of name calling, could you fix me some breakfast? This country air has given me a roaring appetite.''

''Fix your breakfast?'' she screeched.

''That was part of our deal, remember? You cook, I—''

''The deal is off, Mackie. What makes you think I'd stay here with you now?''

''Why is now any different from yesterday when you agreed?''

Last night for one, she thought. And for another, their reminiscent conversation about a shared experience she had hoped he'd forgotten. She wasn't, however, going to cite those reasons.

''There's been too much water under the bridge. This is never going to work. One of us will end up murdering the other.''

''Again, you're demonstrating a real flare for creativity, Stevie. If I get writer's block, I plan on consulting you first." He inspected the refrigerator. "For right now, juice, toast and coffee will do. When we go to the store later today, remind me to buy bacon and eggs."

"*Mackie?*"

He came around. "What? And for future reference, you don't have to shout. I'm not hard of hearing."

"And I'm not staying."

He studied her for a moment, a picture of exasperation. "Fine. The keys to the car are on the hall table. Be careful driving. But before you go, consider this."

He held up his index finger. "One. Your condo will probably still be staked out by the media. The public will be panting to know whether or not you're going after the Grand Slam. Will you play Wimbledon in three weeks or not? Will you have surgery right away or won't you? What are the consequences if you don't? What's your prognosis if you do?"

"Can you give them answers to those questions, Stevie? No. Because those are the questions you're still grappling with yourself. What better place to arrive at some answers than the peace and quiet of the country, far away from the news hounds and unsolicited advisers?''

Another finger went up. "Two. You look like you need a vacation. You've still got unattractive dark circles under your eyes." His ring finger joined the first two. "Three. I got fired on account of you. The least you could do is cook a few meals for me while I try to hack out a rough draft for a novel. Selling it for publication may be my only hope of supporting myself in the future." His pinkie sprang up. "And four, nothing infuriates me more than somebody who goes back on his word."

His reasons made sense, especially the first one, but Stevie glared at him mutinously, still not prepared to surrender unconditionally. "I need to practice. Do you realize how rusty I'll get if I don't play some tennis at least once every day?"

"Valid point." Gnawing the inside of his cheek, he considered their alternatives. "When we drive into town, we'll check the public school. If memory serves me, it's got a tennis court. And since I'm the only famous or near-famous person from around here," he said with a conceited grin, "I think I can finagle permission to use it."

"If you can do that, I'll stay."

"Thank heaven that's settled," he muttered, turning to pour himself a fresh cup of coffee. "I'll be in the dining room writing. You can bring me my juice and toast in there. I like it lightly browned and heavy on the butter."

"The juice or the toast?"

He was almost to the door when he turned and scowled. "Try and not make any distracting noise."

She was tempted to go after him and deliver a good swift kick to his taut, narrow buttocks.

But she didn't.

One evening over dinner, Stevie contentedly remarked that these were halcyon days. Judd gave her a reproving look and said, "You'll never make a writer if you resort to clichés like that."

Despite his teasing, that was the adjective that best described their days. She awoke early and puttered around in the yard. The mint growing near the back porch was thriving. She'd carefully weeded around long neglected, but stalwart, periwinkles, which were now profusely blooming in shades of pinks and purples in front of the house.

On one of their trips into town, she'd bought a package of zinnia seeds. They'd been planted and were already sprouting. She enjoyed watching the vibrant green shoots grow, thriving in the rich east Texas soil. Stevie regretted that she wouldn't be around to enjoy their brilliant blossoms.

Judd was a late and grumpy riser. Each morning he stumbled into the kitchen and poured himself coffee she had brewed. It took at least three cups to make him civil. He then retired to the dining room to work on his novel. Later she would take him toast or cereal, but as often as not when she silently checked from the archway, it was still on the tray, untouched.

After lunch, Judd would return to his typewriter. Stevie napped or read in the afternoons. She studiously avoided thinking about her illness or what she was going to do about it. That was the purpose behind this respite from her normal schedule, but she couldn't bring herself to dwell on it.

At dusk they drove to the public school campus and played low impact tennis, wearing inexpensive shorts they'd bought in the only drygoods store in town, where they had also purchased other clothing. Her new wardrobe had little merit beyond keeping her decently covered, but she had had more fun shopping for it with Judd than she ever remembered having on a buying spree.

They took drives through the countryside in the cool of the evening, or sat together in the bench swing beneath the pecan tree, or played cards on the porch. Judd cheated unconscionably and sulked when he didn't win, blaming his losses on everything from the weak porch light to the racket made by the cicadas in the trees.

One evening he had disgustedly tossed down a losing hand and said, "Let's play strip poker and the winner has to take off all her clothes."

Gloating, Stevie had raked in her mountain of match sticks. "Such a sore loser."

"That's a game I wouldn't mind losing."

His back was propped against one of the posts supporting the roof over the porch. He was lazily wagging his knee back and forth. Even in the faint glow of the porch light, Stevie could see the intensity of his gaze and sensed that he was no longer teasing.

With clumsy hands, she quickly reshuffled the deck and dealt a new hand. "Maybe if you try playing fair instead of cheating, you'll win this hand."

She didn't acknowledge either his suggestion or the fire in his eyes. Doing so could prove dangerous. She had been dancing close to the flame since agreeing to stay alone with him. So far, she had been singed, not burned. She wanted to keep it that way. There were undercurrents between her and Judd that she couldn't cope with. It was easier to pretend they didn't exist.

One afternoon they bought an edition of the *Tribune* at the grocery store. Stevie was crushed when she read the sports page. One of her rivals had won the Lobo Blanco tournament. "They're saying she might replace me as the top-seeded player," she told Judd glumly.

"Ready to go back and face the music?"

She raised her head and stared into his eyes for a moment, seeing in them the same reluctance she felt toward his suggestion. "No. Not yet."

"Me, either." Unable to mask his relief, he playfully jerked the newspaper out of her hands. After a moment of reading, he said, "Look, here's a letter to the editor from a reader asking about me."

"How does the management respond?"

"That I'm taking a 'few weeks off.' "

"They don't come right out and say that you're fired," she said, reading over his shoulder. "That must mean they want you back. Should you call them?"

"No way." He refolded the paper and tossed it aside. "Let Ramsey sweat."

The next morning, the postman delivered a letter to Stevie as she was working in the flower bed. It was addressed to Judd. Wiping her hands on the seat of her shorts, she went inside.

"I hate to disturb you, but a letter just came." She entered the dining room. Judd, she noticed, not for the first time, typed with his index fingers only.

He finished his sentence, then rolled the paper out of the machine and laid it face down on the card table. He had refused to discuss his plot, characters or anything else about his book with her. He never gave her a glimpse of what he'd written and had forbidden her to pick up the wastepaper that littered the floor every morning.

He read the letterhead and muttered scoffingly, "Ramsey." Judd scanned the brief letter, crammed it into a ball and tossed it onto the floor where his other rejections were strewn.

"Well," Stevie asked impatiently, "is he sweating yet?"

"Like a pig. But he hasn't got to the begging stage."

"He has to beg?"

"Sure he has to beg. I want him to get as low as a slug and then grovel."

She laughed. "I take it that means you're not ready to go back."

"What I'm ready for," he said as he came to his feet, "is lunch." He placed his arms around her, clapped his hands on her bottom, gave the firm flesh a hard squeeze and soundly kissed her. "Fetch my food, woman."

She slipped out of his arms, asking saucily, "Or what?"

His eyes became drowsy and as sultry as the summer weather. "Or I'll show you what else I'm ready for."

She fetched his food.

Nine

〜◦ℭ◦〜

"**Y**ou're awfully quiet tonight. Is something wrong?"

Stevie, who had been staring vacantly over their dinner table, blinked Judd into focus. "No, nothing. I'm sorry I'm not better company."

"You're not having any pain, are you?"

She shook her head. "Just tired I think."

"No wonder. You waxed me today on the tennis court."

She smiled, but it was a fainthearted attempt. "You still gave me a good workout."

Watching her closely, Judd played with his spoon, turning it end over end. "It's more than fatigue, isn't it, Stevie?"

"Maybe. I don't know. I've got a lot on my mind."

"It was seeing that couple."

She looked at him sharply, then tried unsuccessfully to hide her spontaneous reaction by innocently repeating, "Couple?"

"The young couple we saw in the grocery store this afternoon. The couple with the baby."

She looked away, which was as good as a signed confession.

"Up till then we'd been having a great time," Judd said. "You beat me soundly in three sets, but I lost gracefully. We were joking, wrestling over the last bite of Hershey bar, doing our grocery shopping."

"Then you caught sight of those two attractive young people wheeling their basket down the store aisle, cooing to the kid and smiling goosily at each other over the top of his curly, blond head. After that, you clammed up and have had the personality of a turnip ever since."

"I didn't know that my duties as cook extended to being a court jester, too," she said caustically. "Maybe you should have specified that."

He dropped the spoon onto the table with a clatter and held up his hands in a gesture of surrender. "Touchy, touchy. It's *you* I'm worried about."

"Well, don't be."

"Too late. I already am."

Stevie gauged his expression. It appeared to be sincere. She wanted, and needed, to believe that it was. With a short, self-derisive laugh, she said, "I suppose you think I'm the one who's goosey."

"Actually that living portrait of matrimonial bliss and domestic harmony left me a little choked up, too."

"I'll bet," she said drolly.

"It did. I haven't always been a surly, cynical jerk, you know. The owners of this house, my grandparents, instilled in my father some basic values. He, along with my mother, instilled a few in me."

"What happened to them?"

"They got dashed against the rocky shore of outrageous fortune."

"I hope you're not putting that in your novel. It's terrible."

His lips tilted into a half smile. "Not in those exact words, but they sort of capture the gist of the theme."

She lifted her shoulders, then let them drop as she released a heavy sigh. "Okay, as long as we're being open and honest, I'll admit that seeing that poignant little scene got to me. I was envious."

"Envious?" he asked incredulously. "How could you be envious of these rural folk? You've traveled the world several times over, been introduced to royalty, earned a helluva lot of prize money in addition to what you make on endorsements. You couldn't possibly build a trophy room large enough to hold all that you've received."

"None of which I can confide my troubles to. I can't curl up with a trophy on cold nights. Or even have a healthy fight with one."

"Know what this sounds like to me? Whining."

"That's exactly what it is," she retorted crossly.

He let a moment go by before asking, "Are you regretting some decisions, Stevie?"

"Yes. No. I don't know, Judd. It's just that..." She paused, trying to convert her random thoughts into understandable language.

"For the past three years, the Grand Slam has eluded me by one tournament. Once I had got it,

I planned to slow down. I would have had to anyway in a year or two because of my advancing age, but I had already decided that if I got the Grand Slam I wouldn't ask for more. I'd retire on top, with dignity and a very respectable career behind me."

Pensively she continued, "But I didn't think much beyond that. Now that the inevitable future is here, it seems so bleak, so empty. There's nothing in it. There's *nobody* in it."

"No baby."

"No baby," she repeated emotionally. "And probably no chance of having one. Ever."

"Do you wish you had had a child sooner?"

"Maybe. But hindsight is twenty-twenty, isn't it?"

"With whom, Stevie?"

She laughed mirthlessly. "Good question. With whom? I never took the time to fall in love, get married, develop a meaningful relationship. I'm not even certain what that catch phrase means or how it applies to me and members of the opposite sex."

"Now that you've got the time to find out, you might not get the opportunity. Is that what's bothering you?"

"In a nutshell, yes."

Each fell silent. Judd was the first to speak. "Sometimes our decisions are forced on us."

"Mine weren't. I freely made my choice years ago. I chose tennis. At all costs, I wanted to be the number one player in the world."

"You are."

"I know. I also know I have no reason to complain. It's all been wonderful." She gave him a bleak smile. "It's just that every once in a while, like today, I'm reminded of everything I sacrificed and start feeling sorry for myself. Now that my career is coming to an end, I'm asking myself, 'now what?'. And I don't have any answers."

She took a deep breath. "In my estimation, self-pity is the most wicked of sins. It's also a big waste of time, unless it's within one's power to bring about a change. In my case," she concluded, laying a hand on her tummy, "I don't have control over the situation. That's the bitterest pill to swallow."

They had finished their meal. Judd helped her clean up the dishes. In that respect, he wasn't nearly as chauvinistic as he pretended to be.

"I'm going on up to bed," she told him as soon as they'd finished the chore.

"To brood?"

"No, because melancholia is exhausting."

He smiled crookedly. "Personally I think there are a lot of sins far more wicked than self-pity. Want me to enumerate a few I've engaged in, just so you'll feel better?"

"Thank you, no. I'll pass."

He pressed her shoulders between his hands and dropped a quick kiss on her forehead. "Say your prayers. And close your door so the typewriter won't bother you."

"It doesn't bother me."

She stood looking up at him, feeling lost and lonely. She wished for something. For what exactly, she wasn't sure. For starters she wished that his good-night kiss had been placed on her mouth rather than her forehead. She wished it had been deep and lingering instead of light and quick. She wished his caress hadn't been so fraternal and that he hadn't removed his hands from her shoulders so soon.

She was seized by a strange and powerful yearning that she couldn't put a name to. It was silent and internal, but as strong and over-

whelming as a waterfall. She longed to rest her
cheek against Judd's chest and feel the safe
sanctuary of his arms closing around her. She
wanted to hear his husky voice whispering en-
couragement into her ear, even if all he gave her
were platitudes.

Before she submitted to the impulses tugging
at her, she needed to put space between herself
and Judd. He might mistake her unnamed need
for weakness. "Good night."

"G'night, Stevie."

She couldn't sleep. The day had been cloudy
and muggy. Ordinarily her room was cool
enough, thanks to the droning oscillating fan
that stirred the evening air. She hadn't missed air
conditioning a bit. Indeed, she liked watching the
sheer curtains on the open windows billow and
float on the breeze.

But tonight the curtains were hanging limply
in the windows. There was no breeze. Even if the
curtains had been doing their entrancing dance,
she doubted it could have lulled her to sleep. She
was restless. Her body needed sleep, but her
mind wouldn't cooperate and let it come.

Suddenly it occurred to her why she couldn't
sleep. Judd's typewriter wasn't clacking. Con-

trary to what he thought, the sound of its metallic tapping didn't keep her awake when he worked well into the early morning hours. It had become a reassuring sound, an indication that for once she wasn't spending the night alone in an otherwise empty house.

Throwing off the light muslin sheet, she padded over to her bedroom door, which was always kept open to allow the air to circulate through the house—a lesson she had learned from Judd, one which he remembered from spending summers on the farm with his grandparents when he was a boy. She listened. Nothing.

A quick peek into his bedroom revealed that he hadn't gone to bed yet. She moved to the head of the staircase and looked down. The light was burning in the dining room. He was still up, probably just taking a break. But she waited for several minutes, and he didn't resume typing.

Curious, and somewhat worried, she crept down the stairs and silently approached the dining room.

She caught him deep in thought. His pose was what she considered to be very "authoresque." He sat, staring at the page in his typewriter, his hands folded over his mouth, elbows propped on the card table.

The sleeves of his white T-shirt had been cut out, though it looked more like they'd been chewed out. The armholes were ragged. He was wearing a pair of navy blue shorts.

His hair looked as though it had been combed with the yard rake she used in the flower beds around the house. One damp, dark lock had fallen over his brow. His feet, in laceless tennis shoes, were resting on the lowest rung of the straight chair. His spine was bowed.

Not wanting to disturb him, she backed away and turned toward the stairs without making a single sound.

"Stevie?"

She came up short and stepped back into the light of the open archway. "I'm sorry. I didn't mean to distract you."

"Obviously you didn't."

"The muses aren't being kind tonight?"

"Those bitches." With his hair falling across his forehead, his face shadowed from above by the lamp on the table and below by his sprouting beard, he epitomized disreputability.

He looked temperamental and dangerous and . . . gorgeous. Something deep inside Stevie stirred and stretched, like a seed that had been planted in fertile soil and was now on the brink of germination.

"Why aren't you asleep?" He took a slurp of coffee she knew must be stone cold.

"I don't know." She lifted her hands awkwardly, then let them drop back to her sides. "I think I missed the sound of the typewriter. And the humidity is oppressive. As long as I'm up, I'll be glad to make some fresh coffee."

"No thanks. I've had enough." He looked her up and down. "You okay?"

"Yes."

"No problems?"

"No."

"I don't believe you. If you were okay, you'd be asleep."

She came farther into the room. Her nightgown had been one of the purchases she'd made in the dry goods store. It was sleeveless, had a tucked-and-pleated lace-trimmed bodice, and was modest enough for a nun. Although a nun probably wouldn't have worn a nightgown made of cotton that was so soft and sheer that light could shine through it.

Unaware that her body was silhouetted against the fabric, she extended her arms at her sides. "See? I'm fine."

"Well, I'm not," he muttered grouchily. "Sit down and keep me company for a while."

She glanced around. "There's no place to sit."

"Sure there is." He swiveled his legs from beneath the table, reached for her hand and pulled her onto his lap.

She felt his bare thighs against the backs of hers. The contrast was so thrilling she uttered a soft cry. "Judd!"

Nuzzling her neck, he snarled, "Did I ever tell you that white cotton nighties make me as horny as hell?"

"No!"

"Well, they don't. I just wondered if I ever told you that."

"Oh, you!" she remonstrated, giving his shoulder a push.

Chuckling, he raised his head, but loosely linked his hands around her waist. His eyes moved over her. "I couldn't seduce you now even if you'd let me."

"Why?"

"Because you look about twelve-years-old, that's why. With your hair down and wearing your sweet, prim nightie."

Smiling, he ran his index finger down the row of tiny buttons until it came up against a neatly tied satin bow between her breasts. By then, he was no longer smiling. He lifted his eyes to hers. Their gaze melded.

Stevie's pulse was pounding in her ears. He had already teased her once about her rapidly beating heart, and she wondered if he could feel it now. She could scarcely breathe.

Before things got out of hand, she had to bring the subject back around to his writing. "Is it terribly hard?"

"It's getting there," he replied roughly.

"How long will it be?"

"Long enough, baby."

"What's it about?"

"Huh?"

"Your book."

"Book? Oh, my book. We're talking about my book."

He dropped his head forward and blew out a pent-up breath. For several moments he breathed deeply with his eyes shut. When he raised his head again, there were lines of strain around his mouth.

" 'Book' is a polite euphemism for 'pile of crap.' " He nodded toward the pages turned facedown on the table.

"I'll bet it's not crap at all. You've been working so diligently, it can't be all bad."

"Hopefully not." He took her hand in his and studied it. Turning it palm up, he ran his thumb across the calluses left by her tennis racquet. His touch was a further aggravation to her already chaotic system and increased her awareness of the warmth emanating from his lap up through her thighs.

Hastily she withdrew her hand and made to stand. His arms tightened around her. "Where are you going?"

"Back to bed."

"I thought you were going to talk to me."

"You're not talking."

"You want to know what the book is about?" he asked moodily. "Alright, I'll tell you."

"I—"

"Hush. You keep bugging me to know, so now you'll know. Be quiet and listen."

Ordinarily Stevie would have protested this gross inaccuracy. Since she had first asked him about his novel and he'd told her that writers didn't discuss their current projects, she had refrained from asking specific questions about it. She usually referred to what he did in the vacant dining room, as his "work."

Now, however, she could tell that he was bursting to discuss certain aspects of it. Obediently she sat silently on his lap and listened.

"It starts out when the protagonist is just a kid, see?"

"Male or female?"

"Male."

"Figures."

"He had a very ordinary—"

"Does he have a name?"

"Not yet. Are you going to keep interrupting? Because if you are—"

"I won't say another word."

"Thank you." He took a deep breath, opened his mouth, then looked at her blankly. "Where was I?"

"May I speak?" His glare threatened murder. She quoted, "'He had a very ordinary...'"

"Oh, yeah. He had a very ordinary childhood. Mom, Dad, typical suburban-America upbringing. He'd always been good at sports. All sports. But in high school, he concentrated on baseball. By his senior year, he'd won the attention of many notable universities, all vying for him. He picked one and got a scholarship in exchange for playing baseball on the varsity team."

"During his sophomore year of college, a minor league talent scout approached him and offered him a contract to go pro. It was as tempting as hell. Although his coaches, everybody, had told him that he had what it took to make the major leagues, he decided that he had better decline—much as he wanted to play—and go ahead and finish college, just in case this career in baseball didn't pan out."

"So he stayed in school, which, as the story progresses, turned out to be one of the wisest decisions he ever made. Since he wasn't particularly interested in any other field, he tried to find the path of least resistance to get through college. He'd never been much of a scholar, too busy with athletics, you see."

"Science and math courses were a hassle for him, and he barely squeaked by. But he aced classes like English and history where he could b.s. his way through an exam. Friends told him that he had a way with words and a knack for turning a clever phrase. So, it seemed logical that he major in English and minor in journalism.''

"By the time he graduated from college, he had an agent negotiating with three major-league teams. Under the misconception that he was invulnerable, he behaved recklessly, thinking that his future was one big bright solar system that revolved around him, its sun. He partied a lot. There were lots of women, good times, fun and frolic.''

Judd fell silent for a moment and stared reflectively at the blank sheet of paper in the typewriter.

"One of those seven-figure, five-year deals that dreams are made of came through for this clown. He was celebrating it with a group of friends. They decided to spend a weekend waterskiing.''

Stevie rolled her lips inward, wishing she didn't have to listen to the rest of the story. But dynamite couldn't have blasted her off Judd's lap. Apparently he desperately needed this catharsis. He had listened on several occasions when she had poured her heart out. It was time she returned the favor.

"The lake had been formed by a new dam and hadn't completely filled up yet. Those kids were stupid to be skiing there in the first place. This fool was even laughing his head off when the boat approached the stump sticking above the surface of the water."

"Hell, he was invincible. Nothing could touch him. Or so he thought," he said in a flat, empty voice. "He decided that he could swerve around the stump without any trouble at all." After a moment, he added, "He couldn't."

The resulting silence was broken only by distant thunder. It rumbled ominously. The sky flickered with lightning; the breeze picked up. But neither Stevie nor Judd noticed these changes in the weather.

"All his big plans were shot to hell," Judd continued. "One dumb move and the course of his life was changed forever. The seven-figure offer was revoked after the doctors told the team management that he'd never be pro material even if they did their best for his leg."

"He never got to play major-league baseball. After a year of reconstructive operations on his busted tibia, he went to work writing about the sports he could no longer play.''

It began to rain. Fat, splattering drops fell onto the flowers that Stevie had so painstakingly cultivated. Rain splashed against the open windows. The curtains were driven into the room by the gusty wind. Lightning crackled and thunder crashed. The air turned noticeably cooler, a welcome relief from the humid heat.

Stevie was unaware of the storm, unaware of everything except Judd. She brushed back the strand of hair that had fallen over his forehead and smoothed out the frown between his eyebrows.

He gave her a twisted grin. ''You won't want to read the book. I don't think it's going to have a happy ending.''

''Why not?''

He slipped his finger into the neckline of her nightgown and slowly traced the edge of the material around the base of her neck. He did it without really thinking about it.

''For years after his accident, the protagonist was mad at the world, even madder at himself for screwing up his life. He went through the motions of living, but just like Rhett Butler, he didn't really give a damn. He worked hard at making everybody around him as miserable as he was himself. He got drunk often, slept with nameless women, picked fights.''

"Fights?"

He shrugged, now toying with the buttons on her gown again by lightly plucking at them. "To prove to himself that the accident hadn't emasculated him. He wasn't a strutting jock anymore.''

"Athletic prowess has never been the true measure of a man.''

"Sell that theory to your average American male.''

She lifted her shoulder in semiconcession, a move that caused his knuckles to make a dent in the inner slope of her breast. "How will the story end, Judd?''

"Ah, that's what's hanging me up. I'm up to the part where he finally settles into a well-paying job, which he goes through the motions of doing, expending as little effort as possible. He's got everybody but himself buffaloed into believing that what he's doing has merit. But what eventually becomes of this guy, who still resents like hell that he blew his one big chance in life?''

"I don't think you're giving yourself enough credit," Stevie remarked in a soft, sympathetic voice. "It takes a tremendous amount of talent to turn out a newspaper column every day. Being prolific is certainly no small thing when journalism is your occupation. Your columns haven't always pleased me, but they're never stale or... What's the matter?"

He was no longer touching her with subconscious, intimate familiarity. His eyes had turned as stormy as the night sky. "Have I said this story is about me?"

His sudden mood shift stunned her. "Well, no, not specifically," she stammered, "b-but I... assumed..."

"The character in my book is dissatisfied with his life. Do I look like a guy who's dissatisfied with his life?"

He stood up, practically dumping her onto the floor. She staggered backward in an attempt to regain her balance. When she did, she glared at him with contempt and fury. He had told her his sob story, but when it came time to accept her compassion, he had turned stupidly, defensively macho.

"What you look like is a joke of a journalist, who is finally getting around to hacking out the dreary novel that he's been claiming for years to have burning inside him to anybody dumb enough to listen to that drivel."

"You don't know anything about me, Miss Cute Buns," he said with a dangerous scowl.

"I know that you're too insensitive to write copy for sardine cans, much less a novel about human emotions and life's disillusionments. Speaking of which," she sneered, gesturing down at the table, "I think the subject matter of your book is self-indulgent and boring."

He took the steps necessary to close the distance between them. Through his clenched teeth he said, "Not if I detail the character's interactions with women."

"In that case, add disgusting to self-indulgent and boring and you've got my critique!"

On that outstanding exit line, she stamped from the room.

Ten

It was still raining the following morning, but it wasn't the sound of thunder that awakened Stevie. It was the cramping in her lower abdomen. The twinges were like menstrual cramps, only more localized and more severe, particularly in her right side.

She got up and took two of her pain pills. Back in bed, she turned onto her side and drew her knees up close to her chest. Eventually the cadence of steady rainfall induced her back to sleep.

She must not have been sleeping very deeply, however. When she awakened again, Judd was speaking her name in gentle inquiry. She felt the mattress dip beneath his weight as he lay down behind her and placed a hand on her shoulder.

"Stevie, what's the matter?"

"Nothing." She lay unmoving, her eyes remaining closed.

"I could hear you moaning all the way in my bedroom. You woke me up."

"I apologize."

He swore beneath his breath and muttered something derogatory about the female psyche. "I don't care about missing out on some sleep," he hissed. "Are you in pain?"

"A little."

"Damn."

"Only a slight cramp. Don't worry about it. It'll go away."

"Where are your pills? I'll get them for you."

"I already took two."

"When?"

"I don't know. Not long ago."

"Why aren't they working?"

"They haven't had time."

"What can I do?"

"Nothing."

"Why are you keeping your eyes closed?"

"Because I'm sleepy." And because she knew, intuitively, that he had come to her bed as he slept in his—naked. "Go on back to bed. I'll be alright."

"Where do you hurt?"

Impatiently she snapped, "Where are my tumors?"

"What would help?"

"My heating pad might."

"Where is it?"

"I didn't bring it."

"Great."

He didn't say anything else, but he didn't go away, either. Stevie could feel him staring down at her. Abruptly, as though he suddenly made up his mind about something that had him in a quandary, he slid his arm around her waist, fumbling through bedding and cotton nightie before his hand found skin.

"Judd! What are—"

"Shh, shh. Lie still. I want to help."

"You can't."

"Maybe not, but I want to try."

"Why?"

"Because I was rough on you last night. I yelled at you and you didn't deserve to be yelled at."

"That doesn't matter. This isn't necessary."

"Look, this Good Samaritan gig is new to me, so give me a break and help me along, okay? Now, where do you hurt? Here?" He placed his warm hand over her lower body, applying just the right amount of pressure.

"Hmm." A soothing heat spread through her, melting away the pain, ironing out the cramps. It felt wonderful.

"Is that better?" He waited. "Stevie?"

She was already asleep.

When she woke up the third time, the weight of his arm was lying heavily in the hollow of her waist. His hand was still palming the area between her hipbones. The pain was gone.

The fingers of his other hand were ensnared in her hair where it mingled with his on the pillow they shared. If he was going to invade her bed, the least he could have done was bring his own pillow, she thought.

Her peevishness was a ruse she employed to convince herself that she didn't like feeling his solid presence along her back, touching from shoulders to toes, nor the warm, damp gusts of his breath against her nape.

She tried telling herself that his body was heavy and intrusive, when actually she relished the feel of it against hers. So much so that she reflexively snuggled closer to him.

Her eyes opened wide when she was alarmingly reminded that Judd's sleeping attire had been chosen for maximum comfort and left no doubt that she was in bed with an extremely virile man. Hoping that she wouldn't awaken him, she turned her head slightly.

He snuffled, stirred and opened his eyes. Their faces were very close. Stevie felt as though the bizarre occasion called for something. A thank-you. A tension-breaking laugh. A reprimand.

She neither said nor did anything, only lay there staring into a rugged, well-lived-in, beard-roughened face that was becoming distressingly dear to her.

When Judd finally moved, it was only to spread wide his fingers against her abdomen and to press it gently with the heel of his hand. Then, moving that hand to the curve of her waist, he slowly drew her onto her back.

His eyes went on a silent tour of her, touching everywhere: her hair, which he was lazily sifting through his fingers, her eyes, her mouth, her throat. He smiled with amusement as they roved down the prim bodice of her girlish nightgown to the satin bow that made it seductive. Gradually his gaze made its way back up to hers.

He moved again, this time to bracket her shoulders with his elbows. He used them to prop himself inches above her. He pressed one of his legs between hers, smooth flesh against rough. His thigh lay warmly and heavily in her cleft.

He took her face between his hands, sliding his fingers up through her hair and curving them around her head. His thumbs made light passes across her lips. They parted. The point of separation seemed to intrigue him, and he investigated it with the tip of his thumb.

Then he lowered his head and replaced his stroking thumbs with a kiss as soft as the summer rain falling upon the leaves of the trees outside.

Reflexively Stevie's arms went around him. She splayed her hands over his broad back. Gaining confidence, she rubbed them up and down, eventually going as far as the dimples in the small of his back.

He released a low, primitive groan and pressed his tongue between her lips. His lips slanted across hers to achieve the best fit and ultimate satisfaction. His tongue probed deeply, masterfully, but unhurriedly. It was a tranquil, sleepy, rainy morning kiss.

It was delicious.

When it was over and they pulled apart, they gazed at each other with drowsy complacence. Strands of her hair had become enmeshed in his stubble. She reached up to pull them away, but he caught the tip of her finger between his teeth and nipped it, then bathed the ball of it with his soft, damp tongue.

She investigated his face with her hands, as one blind, ghosting over the rough, masculine features with curious fingertips. She tried in vain to smooth out the dense eyebrows, though she thought they were incredibly attractive just as they were.

He bent his head and kissed her bare shoulder. She slipped her arms beneath his again and gave him a hard, urgent hug, wanting to feel his weight pressing down on her again.

He granted her wish, readjusting his body against hers for an even more tantalizing match, then slightly rocking them together. His mouth tenderly ate at hers, giving it kiss after kiss— open, hot, wet and deep.

Slowly, taking it one small button at a time, he unfastened her nightgown. When he got to the satin bow, he raised his head and watched as his fingers pulled on one end of the ribbon until it came free. He moved the cotton aside.

Stevie gauged his reaction with trepidation, but there was nothing glowing in his hazel eyes except admiration and desire. His tanned fingers curved around her paler skin, cupping her breast. His expression grew as soft as the flesh he was gently supporting.

But Stevie didn't see that. By now her eyes were closed, and, between parted lips, her breath rushed in and out on shallow pants. Judd nuzzled the breast he held, rubbing it with his nose, his chin, his lips, lightly scratching it with his bearded cheeks. Stevie murmured with want and need, and responsively pressed her thigh against his, tilting her hips up and forward.

He kissed the very center of her breast, then took it between his lips and drew it into his mouth. After suckling her with tempered fervency, he kissed her raised nipple. He flicked it rapidly and lightly with the tip of his tongue.

Sensations exploded in her belly like holiday sparklers. She gave a glad, wordless cry. Judd pressed her femininity with his knee and made a grinding motion against it. She clutched his back, digging into the hard muscles.

He sent his hand beneath the sheet, beneath the nightgown, beneath the brief silk panties to caress softness and warmth and woman.

That's when they heard the knocking on the door downstairs, urgent knocking that couldn't be ignored.

The first words with which Judd greeted the new day were precise and profane.

He practically tore the front door off the hinges getting it open. A sodden delivery man, wearing a dripping yellow slicker, didn't look any happier to be there than Judd was to have him there.

"Took you long enough," the man complained.

"I was in bed."

"Hope you appreciate me coming all the way out here in this." He indicated the downpour that had made a quagmire of the clearing surrounding the house. Stevie's valiant little plants were lying vanquished in the mud like victims of a sea battle.

"Oh, yeah, I'm thrilled to see you," Judd mumbled sarcastically as he scrawled his signature along the dotted line of the receipt.

The delivery man handed him the plastic-wrapped overnight letter, hunkered deeper into his slicker and ran down the porch steps to his waiting van. Judd slammed the front door.

"Who was it?"

"A delivery for me."

"From whom?"

In his querulous mood, he hadn't even thought to check. When he read the return address, he cursed. "Mike Ramsey."

"What is it?"

"How the hell do I know? I haven't opened it yet."

He'd never been this frustrated in his life. There they'd been, in that cozy, rumpled bed, kissing like crazy, temperatures rising, things progressing nicely, and now *this*. He could gladly murder Ramsey for unwittingly interrupting.

He was none too pleased to see that Stevie had quickly dressed. Her eyes looked enormous in her wan face, her expression a blend of apprehension and guilt.

Damn! He still had the taste of her mouth and the feel of her breast on his tongue. Even as enraged as he was over the interruption, all he could really think about was resuming where they'd left off.

But instinct told him that it wasn't going to happen. That's why he was so angry. Given a chance to think about it, to reconsider, to let her passions cool, she had backed out.

There was always an outside chance, however, that he was wrong, Judd thought optimistically.

He took a step toward her where she stood poised, as though for flight, on the bottom stair. He looked at her longingly and spoke her name in a hoarse, aroused voice. "Stevie?"

Wetting her lips nervously, she said, "I'll put on the coffee," and headed toward the kitchen at a pace that could fairly be classified as a run.

Judd waited to follow her until he'd exhausted his repertoire of obscenities. Having spent a majority of his adult life either in a locker room or newsroom, that file cabinet of his vocabulary was extensive.

Wearing only the shorts he'd pulled on before going downstairs to answer the door, he went into the kitchen. Flopping into a chair at the table, he ripped open the cardboard envelope while Stevie stood waiting for the coffee to finish perking.

Judd read the one-page, single-spaced, typed letter, then balled it up and stuffed it into the pocket of his shorts. "How long before that coffee is ready?"

"A few more minutes. What did your editor say?"

"Nothing of importance."

"Then why are you looking so surly?"

"Because I haven't had my coffee yet." He sounded testy even to his own ears. But it wasn't Stevie he was aggravated with. It was Ramsey, the situation, his aroused body that refused to relax. "There are other more... *pressing* reasons for my crankiness, but I don't think you really want to hear the details, do you?"

She gave a quick, negative shake of her head.

"I didn't think so," he said in an undertone.

"Is Mr. Ramsey begging now? Is he as low as a slug and groveling?"

"No."

"Then what does he have to say?"

"Not much."

"What's in the letter?"

Her outcry took him by surprise. Shifting his attention from his straining sex to her, he saw that she was drawn up as tight as a high-octave piano wire and obviously none too pleased with his reticence. "Alright, you guessed. The letter was about you."

The instant he confirmed it, she dropped into the chair opposite his. "What did he say?"

"He informed me that you are missing," he said with a wry smile. "He told me that I was losing out on the hottest sports story so far this year. All any sports fan is talking about these days is Stevie Corbett's mysterious disappearance following her collapse at Lobo Blanco."

The light on the percolator blinked on, indicating that the coffee was ready. Stevie hadn't noticed it, so he got up. Returning to the table with two steaming mugs, he set one down in front of her and sipped at his own before continuing.

"Mike urged, *strongly* urged, that I stop pouting and come back to work immediately. He says that with my network of sources, I should be able to track you down before anybody else gets warm." Smiling into his steaming mug, he added, "He seems to have conveniently forgotten that he fired me."

"What are they saying?"

"Who?"

"All the sportswriters. Surely there've been theories on my disappearance."

"Ah, let's see, Mike mentioned something about suicide and—"

"*Suicide?*"

"That's one rumor, yes, but since your body hasn't been found..." He shrugged. "Another hypothesis is that you're secretly hospitalized somewhere. And there's been mention of an exclusive and revolutionary cancer treatment center in the Bahamas. I've been instructed to forget my novel for the moment and find out which guess about the 'Corbett broad'—and that's a quote—is right."

"He knows about your novel?"

"I've mentioned it off and on."

She had hit the nail on the head during their shouting match the night before. For years he had been telling anybody who would listen about this terrific sports novel he was going to write someday. But someday had just never got around to happening.

Until now. It was here. After many false starts over the years, he was finally into the novel and loving every minute of it. It was gut-wrenching, head-splitting, nerve-racking, ego-deflating work, but the prospect of having to set it aside indefinitely was unappealing.

On the other hand, he had financial obligations—like his expensive European car—that his checking account could cover for about another two weeks, and that was stretching it. He had to make a living to support his writing habit.

The solution to his problem was sitting across his grandma's oak table.

He was right on top of a hot sports story that he could sell to the highest bidder. With that nice, fat nest egg to fall back on, he could kiss Ramsey and the *Tribune* column goodbye, at least temporarily, and work full-time on the book he had to expunge from his system whether or not it was ever published.

"What are you going to do?"

Inadvertently Stevie had voiced the question he was wrestling with himself. She had the sense to look worried. She knew the importance of his decision and the impact it would have on her. She realized how valuable her story would be to the journalist who had an exclusive.

Judd ran his hand down his face. He felt terrible for a variety of reasons. His lower body was persistent in its reminders that it was as yet unappeased. A queasiness had seized his stomach, which he attributed to drinking his coffee too fast, although he knew better. It was the thought of another golden opportunity slipping through his fingers that made him ill.

He answered the only way he could, the only way that felt right. "I'm going back to work."

He saw her swallow hard, but watched with admiration as she lifted her chin a notch. "In Dallas?"

She had guts, alright. He wondered how he'd missed seeing that during all these years that he'd been poking fun at her in his column.

"No. In the dining room."

"You won't...won't tell anybody where I am?"

"It'll remain our little secret for as long as you want it that way."

Her relief was visible. She relaxed her rigid posture. Still, she didn't gush gratitude. She didn't genuflect. "Good," she said simply.

"That will make my life easier, and I'm glad you're not forsaking your novel."

"Last night you said it sounded self-indulgent, boring and . . . what was the other word, disgusting?"

She had the grace to look chagrined. "You provoked me to speak unkindly."

"Speaking of provocative," Judd said, slowly leaving his chair and rounding the table, "this morning was—"

"Judd." She popped out of her chair as though her bottom had discovered a splinter in the smooth wood. "I wanted to explain about that."

He actually felt his face muscles forming his frown. "What's to explain?"

"Why it happened."

"I know why it happened. It's called lust, which according to Webster's is a noun meaning a desire to gratify the senses, bodily appetite, sexual desire, especially as seeking unrestrained gratification."

If the venomous look she shot him was any indication, she didn't think that was cute. "I was disoriented. Those pills are strong. I wasn't thinking clearly."

She was backing away from him, staying just beyond his reach. That angered him as much as her excuse for her passion, which he knew damned good and well had been as all-encompassing as his.

"Oh, I see," he said. "You couldn't desire me unless you were under the influence of a controlled substance. Is that what you're saying?"

"Not exactly."

"Then what? Exactly."

"I don't want to make love with you," she declared curtly.

He barked a short laugh. "Like hell you don't."

That steamed her; he could tell. By now he knew the signs: a suffusion of color in her cheeks, a darkening of her eyes, which were the warm, soft color of expensive scotch but a hell of a lot more intoxicating, a determined lift of her chin.

"My life is in crisis," she said in a tight voice. "So is yours. Neither of us needs a romance right now with anybody, but especially not with each other. Maybe we should have taken our cue from Stockholm and—"

"I did. You were hot and ready for me then, too."

Stevie closed her hands into fists and took a deep breath. "We've only got a few days left before I promised to give my manager an answer. During that time, I think we should keep our friendship strictly platonic."

He drew close and sneered, "Tell that to your glands, baby."

She gasped with outrage, then whirled out of the room and up the stairs. He tore after her and got as far as the staircase before he stopped.

The Judd Mackie who hung out with the guys in bars after ball games and boxing matches was urging him not to be a nerd, to go after her. One kiss, one well-placed caress, and she'd be putty in his hands again, begging for it.

He deserved it, didn't he? Hell, he had given up two weeks' pay on her account, not to mention an outstanding story that would have earned him untold income. If his car got repossessed it would be *her* fault.

He had been hospitable, providing her safe refuge and fresh country air, meanwhile banishing himself from his own life and all the pleasures it afforded him, namely booze and broads.

She had cost him time, trouble and money. Was it asking too much for one roll in the hay?

But the Judd Mackie who knew that one roll in the hay with this particular woman would never be enough and who had promised that her secret was safe, forced him to turn and head for the dining room and the waiting typewriter.

Being honorable was new to him. He was bound to suffer a few growing pains, but figured that if he had any character at all, he could endure a few disappointments.

Slightly more than a "disappointment," his wicked side mocked. It cruelly reminded him how much he wanted her sexually by flashing him a mental image of her breasts, flushed and dewy from his mouth's caress.

Look, he argued with his darker self, *I've never had to coerce any woman into bed with me and damned if I'm going to start with Stevie Corbett. Besides, I'm going to be so immersed in my book, I won't have time to think about sex.*

To which his tormentor cackled, *Tell that to your glands, baby.*

Eleven

It rained steadily for two days, forty-eight interminable hours during which they had to tolerate the weather that kept them indoors, each other's fractious mood, the specter of their thwarted lovemaking—which each wanted to diminish in importance but neither could—and the desire that was as tenacious as the inclement weather.

During mealtimes they hardly spoke because when they did the conversations invariably resulted in arguments. To while away one long afternoon, Stevie drove into town and bought the foods necessary to prepare a special dinner, one that would showcase all her epicurean skills.

That turned out to be the evening Judd chose to write through dinner without taking a break. He asked her to bring him a tray in the dining room. After she had spent hours in the kitchen preparing the sumptuous meal, his simple request was tantamount to a declaration of war. She told him from the arched doorway that he could fix his own damn dinner tray and then go straight to hell.

They had another argument over the bathroom.

"Please don't leave damp towels on the floor," she said snippily.

"I wouldn't have to if you didn't hang every garment you own on the towel racks and curtain rod." He swatted at the damp lingerie dangling over the tub.

"Where am I supposed to hang them up to dry in weather like this?"

"Ever heard of a clothes dryer?"

"I can't dry my underwear in a clothes dryer."

Her incredulous comeback seemed to make no sense to him whatsoever. With a snarl and a curse, he stamped from the bathroom.

"It wouldn't hurt you to shave, you know," she called after him.

"What difference does it make to you?"

So it went until, finally, around noon of the third day, the rain stopped. An hour later the sun came out. Steam rose off the puddles in the yard, making the atmosphere as humid as a South Seas island.

Stevie ventured outside first to inspect her battered flower beds. The new plants lay in the mud, but she was confident that a few hours of sunshine would revive them.

"Are they on the critical list?"

Judd ambled out onto the porch. He was wearing his standard wardrobe—shorts. The only variation from day to day was the color of them. He no longer seemed to have any self-consciousness about his scarred leg. Most of the time he went without a shirt and shoes. Clasping his hands together, he turned them inside out and raised them high over his head in an expansive stretch.

"They'll make it, I think," Stevie said, averting her eyes from the fine line of dark hair that arrowed into his waistband.

"I think I've grown bunions on my backside from sitting so long." He lowered his arms to absently rub that particular part of his splendid anatomy. "Want to play some tennis this afternoon?"

No suggestion had ever sounded so good. She desperately needed a hard, pounding match to work off her frustration. Maybe then she wouldn't feel as though her skin were shrinking around her, making everything inside her body feel tight and constricted.

"By all means," she told him. "Just say when."

"When. As soon as we get into the proper duds."

"And as soon as you shave."

He rubbed his bearded jaw. "You drive a hard bargain, lady." She stood her ground. Chuckling, he conceded. "Okay, okay, I'll shave."

"Fifteen, forty."

Bouncing the ball in preparation for her next serve, Stevie muttered, "I know the score."

"Sorry," Judd said, cupping his ear, "I didn't catch that."

Raising her voice, she repeated, "I said I know the score, thank you."

"You're welcome."

Gnashing her teeth, Stevie executed her toss and caught the descending ball at just the right angle, putting exactly the right amount of spin on it. Judd shouldn't have been able to return it.

He did. Easily. And because she hadn't expected him to, she was caught falling down on the job. She didn't make it to the corner of the court in time and missed the return by a mile.

"My game," he said cheerfully. "That makes it five to four, my serve. And we switch courts."

"I know the rules, Mackie."

She wrenched the top off the water thermos they'd brought along and tilted it to her lips. He had won the first set. She had barely taken the second in a tiebreaker. With this game, he could win the match. The possibility was untenable.

He was a smug, gloating winner who was enjoying rubbing her nose in her defeat. Oh, he was doing it sweetly, but she was suspicious of that guileless grin, which many times during the course of the match she'd wanted to slap off his recently shaven face.

She mopped her face with a towel and dried off the handle of her racquet before walking back onto the court.

"We're in no hurry," he said to her from the baseline, where he'd been practicing his toss. "If you need more rest time, feel free to take it."

Gritting her teeth, she said, "Just play."

"Okay."

He lobbed the ball like a rank amateur, so that his serve was high and had the hang time of a well-executed football punt. It bounced high. Stevie had to back up almost to the fence and that destroyed the timing of her forehand swing. Her return went straight into the net.

"Fifteen, love," Judd chortled.

Stevie threw down her racquet. "What the hell was that?"

"That was a missed shot."

She saw red. "I mean your serve, Mackie."

"What?" He spread his arms wide, all innocence. "You seemed a little tired today, off your game. I thought I'd make it easier for you."

"Don't do me any favors, alright?"

"Alright." Then beneath his breath, but loud enough for her to hear, he muttered, "Geez, and I thought McEnroe was temperamental when his game went to crap."

Stevie tried to ignore him and her own mounting rage, knowing well that it was counterproductive and self-defeating, His serve came in low and hard on her backhand side. She returned it. They enjoyed a rally, but Stevie ended up with the point when her well-aimed overhead bounced directly in front of his feet.

"Fifteen all," she said with a sweet smile.

"Good shot."

"Thanks."

Thinking that she would try a similar shot on the next point, she moved to the net too soon. Judd sent a long backhand into the corner of the court and announced with satisfaction, "Thirty, fifteen."

She tied it up on his next serve. "Thirty all," she called out gaily.

Judd's smile wasn't quite as ingratiating as it had been, she noted with satisfaction. She watched his toss, saw the granite set of his jaw, saw his arm go back then arc forward. But just before he hit the ball, he said, "You forgot to wiggle."

The ball whizzed past her like a missile, bounced in the corner of the service court and landed against the fence with a solid *thwack*. Stevie rounded on her complacent opponent, who was inspecting the strings of his racquet.

"What was *that*?"

"That was an ace, something that doesn't get pulled on you very often."

She marched toward the net, a study in fury. 'I'll tell you something else that doesn't get pulled on me. I've never played anybody who opened a conversation just as he was serving the ball. Nobody I know would resort to such a dirty, underhanded trick. Nobody but you, that is. What did you say, anyway? Something about a wiggle?''

"I said you forgot to wiggle."

She propped her hands on her hips. "And what, pray tell, does that mean?"

"Aw, come on, Stevie. We're alone here. We can be open with each other." He leaned across the net and gave her a knowledgeable wink. "I was referring to that little wiggle you give your backside every time you win a point."

Her mouth dropped open. "I have no idea—"

"Sure you do. You do it all the time. It's to make certain that everybody watching, whether from the stadium bleachers or on television, realizes that you've just done something swell."

It took an act of will to stop grinding her teeth. "I don't have to stand out here in this heat and listen to your insults." Reflexively she lifted her long braid off her chest and tossed it over her shoulder.

Judd aimed the handle of his racquet at her like an accusing finger. "That's another one."

"Another one what?"

"Another one of your cuteisms. The one with the braid is to show your degree of frustration either with yourself, your opponent or a line judge."

"Cuteisms?"

He flashed a proud grin. "I coined the word to encompass all the mannerisms you use to draw attention from your game to yourself. Since the way you look is irrelevant to the way you play, you're very clever to use such a tactic."

Stevie was too furious to speak. If she tried, she'd only succeed in sputtering incoherently. She turned her back to him and marched toward the parked car.

"Aren't we going to finish the match?"

"No!"

"You're quitting when it's match point?"

"Yes!"

"Why, because I'm about to beat you?" he taunted, falling into step behind her. "You couldn't stand being beaten by me, could you?"

"I'm having an off day. You said so yourself. It's the heat. I haven't practiced in days."

"Neither have I," he pointed out uncharitably. "And it's just as hot on my side of the court."

She slung her gear into the back seat of his car and got into the passenger side, slamming the door. He got behind the wheel and drove while she sat beside him, fuming in hostile silence.

The pressure had been steadily building. They had been working up to this fight for days. Erroneously Stevie had thought she would welcome a full-fledged blowout as a means of clearing the air. But she was far from having a good time. Probably because Judd definitely had the upper hand in this argument.

"There's nothing wrong with being a showman."

They were more than halfway home before he made that seemingly innocuous observation. It was enough to send Stevie's simmering temper skyrocketing.

"You don't get to be a top-seeded player by being cute, Mr. Mackie."

"Calm down. I'm not going to tell anybody that I beat you."

"You didn't!"

"Only because you refused to finish the match like the spoiled brat you are."

"You weren't playing tennis," she shouted. "The points you scored were scored by playing badly, not well. You were making a mockery of me and of the sport. Your game had nothing to do with talent, skill or finesse." Wanting to drive the next point home, she turned her head to look at him. "The same goes for your writing."

He brought the car to a jarring stop in front of the house. "What the hell is that supposed to mean?"

"You figure it out."

Leaving her things in the car, she got out and bounded up the porch steps. They hadn't bothered with locking the front door. She sailed through it and headed for the stairs. She had almost reached the top when Judd, taking the steps two at a time, caught up with her and grabbed hold of her braid.

"Ouch! Let go of me."

"Uh-uh. Not until you explain that last crack about my writing. What do you mean by saying that I lack talent and skill, etcetera?"

"I didn't say you lack them. There's just no evidence of them in your column."

"I graduated with a degree in journalism, remember?"

"What you print every day isn't journalism, it's gossip," she said, warming to her topic. "Anybody with an inferiority complex and an ax to grind could write what you do. So could anybody who wanted to avoid a real job by boozing it up every night and calling it research. Not to mention the womanizing."

"I haven't touched a drink since we got here. And as for womanizing..." He encircled her waist with his arm and yanked her hard against him. "I haven't done any of that since I left Dallas, either."

"Let me go."

"No way, baby. I've earned this kiss."

His mouth came down hard upon hers. She resisted by bowing her back, which only brought her up harder and higher against him. She tried to free her lips, but he captured her jaw in one hand and held her head steady while his tongue plumbed her mouth repeatedly.

Their breathing was harsh and loud in the otherwise silent house. The sounds of strenuous denial that Stevie uttered deep in her throat diminished to whimpers of desire. Her hands, which had been trying to push him away, began clutching handfuls of his damp tennis shirt. She angled her head, giving his lips better access to hers. Her tongue joined his in love play.

He raised his head suddenly and peered into her wide, dazed eyes. "Stevie?"

"What?"

Taking her hand, he slid it down his body and pressed it against the distended fly of his tennis shorts. "It wouldn't be fair of you to start something you don't intend to finish, would it?" She shook her head and reflexively squeezed the rigid proof of how much he wanted her. "Oh, God." Groaning, he gave her another searing kiss.

Pent-up frustration erupted in an explosion of sexual desire. Their arms wrapped tightly around each other. Their kisses were carnal, ravenous.

Still clinging to each other, they stumbled into the nearest bedroom, his. Blindly he reached for the switch of the ceiling fan. It began to rotate over their heads and cast flickering shadows on the walls as they worked off shoes and bent to remove their socks. They bumped heads but barely noticed in their haste.

He whipped his T-shirt over his head. Stevie did the same. He reached for the front clasp of her bra and unfastened it, shoving the lace cups aside. He touched her briefly, feathering her nipples with his fingertips, making them instantly stiff.

Eyes trained on them, he unzipped his shorts and let them drop. Stevie shrugged off her bra and removed her shorts. Judd, with some difficulty and a near-comical grimace, removed his jock strap.

Stevie couldn't bring herself to glance down, though she wanted to. She hooked her thumbs into the elastic of her panties, but couldn't bring herself to take them off, either. She looked up at him with silent appeal.

"That's good enough for now," he whispered taking her hand and pulling her toward the bed.

He lay down on his back and pulled her on top of him. Cupping her head between his hands, he gave her a long, thorough kiss, sending his tongue deep into her mouth. His legs sawed restlessly against hers. One knee insinuated itself between her thighs and worked its way up until she was riding it.

With one hand, he began tugging her underpants down over her hips. Then he rolled her onto her back and removed them completely. His eyes swept her hungrily. His hands skimmed the surface of her body, touching her breasts, nipples, thighs, the cluster of curls covering her mound.

"Stevie," he mumbled thickly before levering himself above her and pressing his face into the cover of her shoulder.

"Judd?"

"Yes, sweetheart, right now."

"Maybe you should know—"

"I do know, baby. Believe me, I do."

"I'm a virgin."

Twelve

His head popped up. Eyes that had been foggy with passion came into sharp focus as instantly as a high-tech camera.

"A *what*?"

Even after she repeated the word, he stared at her with patent disbelief. Slowly he eased himself up, rolled over to his side and sat on the edge of the bed, keeping his back to her.

"God, I wish I hadn't quit smoking."

He rested his face in his hands, digging into his eye sockets with the pads of his fingers. Eventually he peered at her over his shoulder. She had self-consciously pulled the bedspread over her.

"How did you wind up a virgin?" She gazed at him with puzzlement. "I'll rephrase. Why, *how*, are you still a virgin?"

"Maybe you should have finished what you started in Stockholm."

"With Presley Foster breathing down my neck? No thanks. Did he scare off all your would-be lovers?"

"In fairness to him, no. I did. Not overtly," she added when he gave her a curious look. "I just never took the time to let anything develop. Potential boyfriends always took second place to tennis."

"Second place isn't a healthy or desirable spot for a man's ego."

"So I discovered." She moistened her lips nervously. "I wouldn't have told you if I'd known you were going to stop."

"I wouldn't have gone so far if you had told me sooner."

"Does it matter that much?"

He laughed hoarsely, humorlessly. "Yeah, it matters. A lot."

"Why? I don't think it would have mattered in Stockholm."

"Maybe, maybe not. But in Stockholm I was young and stupid. Now I'm old and stupid. At least when you're young and stupid you've got an excuse for being stupid."

Stevie closed her eyes briefly, then she stretched out her arm and laid her hand on his bare shoulder. "Please, Judd, come back."

Keeping his eyes averted, he stubbornly shook his head no. "I can't assume that responsibility, Stevie."

"It doesn't come with obligations."

"They're implied."

"Not to me."

"To me."

"Please."

"I said no."

A small, strangled sob escaped her.

Judd's head snapped around. He saw her tears, saw the pleading in her eyes. Apparently they touched him in a way her temper tantrums could not. The resolution keeping his lips compressed and uncompromising deserted him. His features softened.

He lay down beside her again and drew her against him. "Don't cry, Stevie. Don't." Typically a cynic where women's tears were concerned, he held her close and kissed her brow with commiseration.

She nuzzled his naked chest, rubbing her face against the pelt of crinkling hair. "Please, Judd, make love to me while I'm still whole. I want it to be you."

"Why?"

"Sentiment, maybe. Even though you doubt it, I know it would have happened in Stockholm if Presley hadn't stopped us." She touched his nipple with the tip of her tongue, licking it deftly, and pressed her palm against his hot, swollen flesh.

"Oh, baby," he moaned, threading his fingers up through her hair. "Stop."

"I don't want to stop."

"You've got to, or—"

"I want to be a complete woman once. Just once, Judd, please."

She dusted his chest with soft, airy kisses, swinging her head back and forth as she worked her way down. She kissed his stomach, then his belly, which was rapidly rising and falling. Her lips tracked the satiny stripe of hair that fanned out denser and coarser on his lower body. He was in a state of supreme agitation and had almost reached the point of no return when he closed his fingers around her head and raised it.

He rolled her to her back and leaned over her. "Okay," he rasped breathlessly, "if you're sure."

"Absolutely sure." He nodded grimly. Laughing, she touched the corners of his mouth. "Your frown is death to my ego. You could look a little happier about it."

"I'm worried."

"I told you not to be. There are no strings attached."

"It isn't that."

"Then what?" Her eyes rounded and she gasped. "You *do* know how, don't you?" she asked teasingly.

"Yeah, I know how," he said, his intensity unchanged. "And hard and fast isn't the way to do it the first time. If you keep doing stuff like that..." He blew out a breath and shook his head as though to clear it. "I'm going to set the tempo. Got that?"

She nodded obediently, though she wasn't sure she could keep such a rash promise when her blood was surging through her veins with a mix of want and wonder. She wasn't sure Judd could stick with the plan, either. His breathing wasn't any steadier than hers and his face was ruddy with arousal.

"Alright, kiss me," he instructed her huskily. "Forget everything you've ever heard about technique. Kiss me the way you think a 'bad girl' would and we'll both have a much better time.''

Taking his advice as a challenge, Stevie linked her arms around his neck and drew his head down. His open mouth met hers, and it was a melding of dual passions. His tongue probed the soft, wet heat of her mouth, sliding in and out, mating with her tongue, which then returned the favor to him, apparently to his satisfaction, for he groaned with pleasure and drew it deeper into his mouth.

His hands rubbed her back, then gradually pulled the bedspread from between them until they were lying naked face to face again. She felt the warm, smooth tip of his shaft against her belly. His thighs pressed against hers. Her breasts lay lush and full against his hard chest; her nipples nestled in the dark, curly hair.

All the sensations were exquisite. The contact with his raw masculinity made her feel wholly female. She wondered how she had survived this long without being intimately acquainted with his body.

And she realized at that moment that she was falling madly in love with her enemy.

Asking him to make love to her had little or nothing to do with Stockholm or with sentiment, or any other excuse she could have conjured up. She wanted to be with Judd, be a part of him, entirely, without reservation or inhibition. It was as simple as that.

Though, actually, it wasn't simple at all. It was very complex. Too complex to muddle through while his mouth was inching down her throat.

He scooped her breast toward his descending mouth and sucked on the tip with strong, urgent tugging motions that touched off responsive chords in her womb. "Ah, Judd," she cried in ecstasy.

"You're sweet, Stevie. Very sweet." He moved to her other breast while his fingers caressed the nipple he'd just left wet and erect.

"Please," she gasped moments later as his tongue feathered one stiff crest. She thrust her hips forward, grinding them against his rigid manhood.

Moaning low, he smoothed one hand down her body and between her thighs. He caressed her gently, moving his fingers between the velvety folds. "Almost, but not quite," he told her, smiling gently into her face before lowering his head and kissing her stomach.

His hands stroked the insides of her thighs, urging them to separate, though without any hint of threat, coercion or violation. He nipped her skin lightly with his teeth and bathed her navel with his tongue.

She cried his name sharply when he kissed the cluster of pale curls between her thighs. Then his tongue, soft and inquisitive and agile, entered her. He kissed her deeply, again and again, until her head was thrashing on the pillow and her body was quickening to the strokes of his tongue.

Rapturously she submitted to the spirals of sensation that were winding her being tighter and tighter. At the height of her release, she clutched handfuls of his hair and gasped his name.

A film of perspiration had broken out on her face when he raised himself above her. He sipped at it while he positioned himself between her thighs and lifted her hips against his.

Holding her there, he pressed into her by slow degrees, letting her body gradually adjust to his hard length, so that by the time he was buried snugly inside her, the only difficulty either had experienced was in holding back the passion that demanded immediate fulfillment.

"You feel wonderful surrounding me," he whispered, softly kissing the lips she had bruised with her own teeth. He swallowed hard and squeezed his eyes shut for a moment, reveling in the ecstasy of being inside her. "You feel sensational."

She murmured his name in a breathy voice while her fingers ghosted lovingly over his face. She was unaware of the tears that glistened in her eyes, but he saw them.

"Are you okay?"

She nodded her head quickly. "Yes, yes, yes."

"Well, I'm not," he said, baring his teeth. "I'm about to die. But, God, it's a helluva way to go."

He began moving inside her, stroking her until they were both senseless and all that mattered was succumbing to the tumult of emotion that seized them. When they did, he pressed his forehead upon hers and chanted her name.

"Want me to—"

"No."

Judd chuckled. "You didn't let me finish."

"Whatever it is, I don't want you to do it because you'd have to move. And if you move, I'll have to," she said, yawning listlessly, "and I don't think I can."

Judd did move, but only to pull her into the circle of his arms and prop his chin on the top of her head. Stevie moved, too, curving her arm around his waist.

"Why did you taunt me on the tennis court this afternoon?" she asked.

"Because you were playing poorly, and the reason you were was that you didn't consider me a worthy opponent and, therefore, weren't putting forth any effort."

"I was playing poorly, yes, but not because I didn't consider you a worthy opponent."

"Then why?"

"My head wasn't in the game."

"Where was it?"

"Here."

"Here?" Judd angled his head back. "You mean here, like we are now?"

"Hmm."

"You just won't let me lie, will you?" he said around a resigned sigh. "In all honesty, that's the reason I was taunting you." Stevie lifted her head off his chest and looked up at him, her expression questioning. "Making love to you is all I've thought about since the other morning when we were interrupted."

"Me, too."

"All you had to do was ask, lady."

"I did."

He looked chagrined. "Oh, yeah, you did, didn't you? Well, you know what I mean."

Smiling, she returned her head to his chest and began idly plucking at the hairs tickling her nose. "I can't believe I'm lying here like this with you, naked and sated. I've often thought that if I ever got you alone, I'd kill you slowly."

He placed his lips close to her ear. "If you hadn't come when you did and given me the green light, you might have succeeded." She giggled and gave his buttock a hard pinch. "Imagine the headlines," he went on, undaunted, "'Famous Tennis Pro Screws Famous Sportswriter to Death.'"

"Will you behave? This is serious. I don't think you realize how badly your nasty articles have wounded me."

His soft laughter subsided. "Why didn't you just consider the source and blow them off?"

"Because almost everything you've written about me is true."

His hand ceased strumming her spine. He eased her off him, placed her on her back, and rolled to his side. Propped on one elbow and leaning over her, he asked, "What are you talking about?"

"Off-the-record?"

"In journalistic circles, when the interview*er* is in bed with the interview*ee* in a state of undress and sexual repletion, it's generally understood that whatever is said is unprintable."

"Oh. Thank you for clarifying that."

"You're welcome. Now quit stalling and run that by me again. What do you mean, everything I've written about you is the truth?"

"A lot of it was. You've often said that I don't belong on a tennis court. In a way, you're right, Judd. From the very beginning my father discouraged me from playing because tennis was 'a rich kid's sport.' I played anyway, but what he had said stuck with me. It gave me a complex. I wasn't like the other players. I wasn't as . . . as *privileged.*"

"That's nonsense."

"Maybe, but that sense of inferiority compelled me to prove myself. I had to work harder at it than anyone else, always playing catch-up. I was accepted into most clubs because of my ability on the court, not my pedigree.

"I always had to be better," she stressed, making an appeal for his understanding, "because acceptance depended on it. That's why, when I was financially able, I always dressed well and played up to the spectators. Don't you see, Judd? I was saying, 'Hey, look at me. I'm worthy of your attention.' I was desperate to win approval. And, yes, sometimes I even resorted to being cute just to ensure that I wouldn't be ignored.

"You saw through all my machinations," she told him in a voice husky with emotion. "You had me pegged from the very beginning. Your columns struck terror in me because they were so incisive. I feared that if my insecurities were visible to you, they must be to everyone else. I'm the classic sufferer of the impostor syndrome. You were my worst nightmare, the person who would expose me."

His eyes were fixed on her lower lip, but he

wasn't contemplating its sexiness so much as he was arranging his own thoughts.

"If all that is true, Stevie, it was an accident. If I tapped into your insecurities, it was by chance and had nothing to do with incisiveness. Fact is, I took digs at you because I resented that a cute, young thing like you could do what you did so well and reach the pinnacle of your sport, when I'd had to fall back on writing about how others were doing what I wanted to do myself. Hacking out that dumb column is a far cry from a career in professional baseball."

"It is not dumb," she said, laying a sympathetic hand along his cheek. "I only said it showed no talent or finesse because I was angry. You've cultivated a faithful reading audience that wouldn't miss a single acerbic word. No writer can do that for any length of time unless there's substance behind his writing. Your readers aren't fools, you know."

"Thanks for the compliment." He finally surrendered to the temptation and kissed her lower lip. "But I know, deep down, that I haven't done a single worthwhile thing since I had that water-skiing accident."

His hazel eyes became dark and intent. "Not until I brought you here. Maybe I've redeemed myself for all the jealousy I've harbored against you."

"Jealousy?"

"Of you and every other pro who made it. I've been lashing out at all of you to some extent, but you were the easiest one to single out."

"Why?"

"Because you were atypical. You weren't muscle-bound and unattractive, which was my chauvinistic, narrow-minded opinion of what a professional woman athlete should look like.

"And," he added around a deep breath, "as long as I'm baring my soul, I might just as well go all the way. I was still miffed about Stockholm. I wanted to go to bed with you, didn't get to, so I was sulking like the little boy who didn't get his candy. Maliciously I disparaged the very thing I desired. Pretty juvenile, huh?"

"Pretty human."

"You're being generous."

"I'm in a generous mood." She smiled up at him and drew a line down his nose with her fingertip. "To prove just how generous, I'll forgive you every nasty word you've ever written about me on one condition."

"What?" he asked suspiciously.

She whisked a kiss across his lips. "Make love to me again."

"Stevie, we really shouldn't."

"Why not?"

He hesitated, which was a mistake. She took advantage of his indecision by sliding her hand down his middle and cupping the full heaviness of his manhood.

"We shouldn't because it might...uh—" he became hard beneath her rhythmic stroking "—might not be good for you," he finished lamely.

"I'll be the judge of that." Her lips nibbled at his chin, her teeth making scratching sounds against his stubble. Her hand became even more persuasive, her thumb lazily inquisitive. "Please, Judd," she breathed against his lips.

Moaning, he clasped her around the waist and pulled her on top of him. "Well, since you asked so nicely...."

Thirteen

Insects gave up their lives against the windshield of Judd's stolen car. The gooey smudges they created made little difference to the thief who could barely see the markings on the interstate highway through her tears.

Stevie wiped her nose on her sleeve. After seventy-five miles she would have thought her supply of fresh tears would be exhausted, but it wasn't. Each time she thought of what she had left behind and the ordeal that she was facing, another hot, salty batch filled her red, swollen eyes.

She had left him and he'd been furious.

Even now, her heartache was overshadowed by the fear that Judd might somehow catch up with her. Glancing once over her shoulder as she had sped away from the farmhouse, she had glimpsed him, wearing only his underwear, running down the porch steps. His fist had been raised. He was cursing her and the rock that had gouged his bare heel.

It could have been a comic sight; it hadn't been. It had broken her heart, and it was still broken. She rather imagined that it would remain broken for a long time.

The skyline of Dallas was glittering and glitzy against the western horizon, deep indigo now in the waning dusk. In an hour she would be at her condominium, she calculated mentally. Allow an hour to make necessary phone calls and pack. Then . . .

She refused to think beyond that. The only way she would get through this alone, without jeopardizing her sanity, would be to take it one step at a time. First things first. Getting home was first.

As she took the exit in the concrete labyrinth that connected one expressway to another, she permitted herself to reflect on their afternoon of lovemaking.

Judd, speaking softly and sexily. Judd, his hands instructive and sensuous, guiding her hips down over him. Judd, hard and full and smooth, filling her. Judd, his lips hungry, yet tender, on her breasts. *Judd, Judd, Judd.*

She dashed tears out of her eyes as she switched lanes cautiously, unaccustomed to driving a sports car with an engine powerful enough to fly an airplane. He would never forgive her for "borrowing" it without his permission. He would never forgive her for leaving him stranded, either.

The farmhouse's old-fashioned bathtub had become a shrine in which they'd worshiped each other's bodies. Hands covered with soapy lather were the sexiest instruments ever employed to give carnal pleasure. Or was it that Judd just knew how to use them?

It had been a delight to discover that the undersides of her upper arms were particularly susceptible to open-mouthed kisses and that kisses to the backs of her knees left her weak.

Judd had a ticklish spot midway between his lowest rib and his right hipbone. He had a birthmark on his left shoulder blade, and he'd grown misty-eyed when she traced every inch of the ugly, jagged scars on his leg with her loving lips.

This has always been an object of fantasy for me, he had confessed, tugging lightly on her long, single braid.

Really?

Really.

How? He had only smiled mysteriously and demurred from telling her. *Then show me.*

Her seductive suggestion had turned his eyes smoky. When he acted out his fantasy with her full cooperation, their harmonious cries of fulfillment had echoed off the walls of the house.

That was the instant she knew unequivocally that she loved him, and her decision had dawned crystal clear. The solution to her dilemma had unexpectedly risen out of the murky depths of confusion and despair.

Life, in its simplest, most basic form was far more precious than any amenities it could afford, such as prizes and fame, respect and riches, the acceptance of either peers or strangers.

While Judd was still dressing, she had gone downstairs, ostensibly to prepare them a light supper. Instead she had grabbed her purse, taken his car keys, and left the house at a dead run, not so much because she feared his wrath over her deception and desertion, but because she feared that given time to think about it, she would change her mind.

She had got as far as the edge of the clearing before he ran out onto the porch, shouting after her, "What the hell? Stevie, come back. Where are you going?" Then, when he realized that she was escaping in their only means of transportation, he'd become furious.

"Damn you, what kind of stunt is this? Ouch! Hell!" Livid, he had cursed when he stepped on the stone. "When I catch up to you, I'll strangle you for this. Dammit," he had sworn, slamming one fist into his other palm.

Her condominium was dark. She was relieved to see that there was no one lurking about. Either the news hounds and merely curious had tired of their siege or had given up on Stevie Corbett altogether.

Her plants needed her immediate attention. She chided herself for forgetting to call the service that took care of them in her absence and vowed to do so at her earliest convenience, though God knew when that would be.

Her first telephone call went to her gynecologist, who was so glad to hear from her that he was nearly incoherent with relief.

"If I don't do it now, I might change my mind." She spoke so quickly that the words stumbled over each other. "I can be there in an hour. Can you make the arrangements that soon?"

He promised he could and would. The next call she made was to her manager.

"Stevie, thank God. I've been frantic."

"I needed time alone to think." She hadn't been alone, but Judd was too complicated to explain, even to herself. "I'm checking into the hospital tonight. The surgery is scheduled for tomorrow morning."

A significant pause ensued. "It's your decision, of course," he said.

"Yes, it is. My life is in the balance. That's more important than a career."

"Hey, it's only Wimbledon," he said with false cheer. "They have it every year. Next year it belongs to you."

They both knew better, but Stevie tried to inject enthusiasm into her voice when she said, "You'd better believe it."

He promised to notify everyone concerned and to issue a statement to the press, which had been having a field day speculating on her whereabouts.

"That's fine, but hold off until tomorrow after the surgery, okay? No matter what the outcome, we'd just as well tell them everything at once." He agreed before hanging up.

After the connection was broken, Stevie felt terribly alone. The silence in her house was depressing, so accustomed was she to hearing the pecking noise of Judd's typewriter in the background.

The framed photos on the walls, picturing her holding aloft trophies of victory, seemed to jeer at her. Memorabilia of her career mocked her from bookshelves and étagères. The prize from The French Open, so recently acquired, no longer seemed to belong to her.

"Too late to reconsider now," she reminded herself as she went into her bedroom and began packing a small suitcase. Then, like a prayer, she whispered, "Stevie, your life is in God's hands."

God had a lot of helpers.

At least there were innumerable people who got their hands on her before she ever made it to the operating room the following morning. By then she had been stripped of all dignity and privacy.

Leaving Judd's car locked in her garage—it wouldn't do to have it stolen twice in one day—she was conveyed to the hospital by taxi.

In Admittance, she had to attach her signature to an endless number of insurance forms, as well as to a note to Jennifer. "My twelve-year-old daughter wants to grow up and be exactly like you," the star-struck receptionist told her.

From there she was taken to be x-rayed. Wearing nothing except a paper poncho, she was placed in a room as cold as a meat locker and instructed to wait, which she did for over an hour before an unapologetic technician came in to x-ray her lungs.

"There, that wasn't that bad, was it?" another technician asked as he slipped the syringe from her vein, from which he'd drawn what looked like a quart of blood. "You can relax now," he said, working her fingers out of the tight fist she'd formed. "Did I hurt you?"

"No," she replied gruffly. "I just don't like needles."

She was finally placed in a private room, but was granted little privacy. A stiff, no-nonsense nurse came swishing in with a sheaf of yet more forms to be signed. "They showed you the video tape downstairs?" she asked dispassionately. "Did you understand it?"

"Yes." The tape had explained all the things that could go wrong during abdominal surgery, each possibility more terrifying, irreversible and deadly than the last.

"Sign here, here and here."

The hospital chaplain came in next. "You're the celebrity in our midst," he said, flashing a glorious smile. After discussing the best remedy for tennis elbow, they bowed their heads over their clasped hands. He prayed for the skilled surgeon and her full, rapid recovery.

Stevie prayed for Judd's stone-bruised heel, forgiveness for stealing his car, protection from strangulation when he caught up with her and for a lawsuit against the hospital on her behalf if she should die on the operating table. She thought somebody should hold the institution accountable even if she'd signed forms absolving it of responsibility.

Her gynecologist came in next and explained the surgical procedure. "If the tumors are benign, and I have every reason to believe that they are, we'll remove them and you'll be as good as new."

"And if they're not?"

"Probably a complete hysterectomy, followed by treatment."

"What kind of treatment? Radiation?"

He patted her hand. "Let's get through the surgery first. Then if we have to discuss options, we will."

The anesthesiologist, who disturbingly reminded her of Count Dracula because of his steep widow's peak, came in and sat down on the edge of her bed. "First thing in the morning, you'll be given a sedative. We'll put in two IVs, one in your arm, the other on the back of your hand."

"I don't like needles," she said in a choked voice.

"I promise to send in my painless assistant. By the time you reach the operating room, you'll be drowsy. Sleep well tonight."

Sleep well? What a joke. She was cleansed from the inside out—a humiliating experience—and given a shot to make her sleepy. She refused anything to eat, even though it had been lunch-time that day since she'd had a bite.

Didn't any of these efficient ghouls realize that she couldn't possibly go to sleep without the distant and reassuring sound of Judd's typewriter?

But he was miles away, stranded in the farm-house. What if it caught fire and he couldn't get away? What if it began raining hard enough to cause a flash flood and he had no means of escaping high water? She tortured herself with hideous possibilities.

She must have slept, however, because when she was awakened by a smiling nurse, she was dreaming that Judd was chasing her with a foot-long hypodermic needle that was shaped like a tennis racquet, laughing maniacally and sneering that he'd teach her the consequences of stealing his car.

In a remarkably short time, she was prepped for surgery and, feeling like a pitifully abused pincushion, wheeled into the operating room. Where last night the hours had seemed to drag by, now everything accelerated to a rapid clip that panicked her. The surgeon squeezed her hand reassuringly and smiled from behind his mask.

"Everything is going to be fine, Stevie. Just relax now. Take deep breaths and start counting backward from ten."

Ten. *She wanted to halt things.* Nine. *She needed more time to think.* Eight. *She needed Judd.* Seven . . .

She weighed ten thousand pounds and these morons were ordering her to scoot across the bed. "That's it, roll to your other side, Miss Corbett. No, don't pull on your IVs. Just relax your arm. That's fine. Right there. Your operation is over."

"Is her catheter in?"

"Yes."

"Isn't her hair pretty?"

"Hmm. Ever seen her play?"

"Are you kidding? I can't afford the tickets."

"I meant on TV. Miss Corbett, did you hear me? Your operation is all over."

Clatter and clank of metal. Jarring motion. Light. So much light. Too bright. Telephones and activity and racket. Why didn't they just be still and quiet and let her sleep?

*   *   *

"Time to turn over again, Miss Corbett."

A groan. Her groan. No, don't make me move. A monster in green scrubs was insisting that she cough.

"Cough, Miss Corbett. Come on now. You've got to cough to clear your lungs." Let them stay clogged. "Miss Corbett. Cough."

She made a feeble attempt just so they'd leave her alone. Her reward was to have something very cold crammed between her thighs. " . . . to keep the swelling down." Someone jarred her bed again. Klutzes. They were all klutzes.

Her hand was tucked beneath the nurse's arm while she pumped the bulb of the blood pressure gauge. "That's good." The binding pressure around her arm was removed. "Miss Corbett, we've got to change your ice pack now."

"A drink?" Her mouth was sprouting cotton.

"You can have an ice chip."

A spoon, cold and hard, was crammed against her teeth, jarring her whole body. Precious ice. She sucked greedily.

"There, just that one. Turn over."

"I can't."

"Sure you can. Cough for me again."

"No."

"Cough." She did. "Good girl. And here's a fresh ice pack."

Thanks for nothing. My thighs are already numb.

" . . . can't come in here!"

"I'm in."

Stevie was aroused by the familiar voice, but opening her eyelids was nigh to impossible. Had they weighted them down with something, fifty-cent pieces like they did corpses in Western movies?

"Visitors are only allowed in Recovery every odd hour at ten till. That's the rule."

He told her what she could do with her rule and his suggestion wasn't very nice. "I'm going to see her whether you like it or not."

"I'm calling security."

"Stevie?"

"Judd?" she croaked.

"I'm here, baby."

A strong, warm hand clasped hers. She whispered, "Are you going to strangle me?"

"There he is, officer. He's not supposed to come in until ten till the hour."

"Later, baby."

A soft whisk of his lips across her forehead then he was gone.

It was probably just another bizarre dream.

"You're sure?"

"Positive."

"You took out everything even potentially dangerous?"

"Everything."

The doctor noticed that his patient's eyes were open and that she was solemnly regarding him and her disheveled visitor.

"You're doing fine, Stevie," he told her with his bedside smile firmly in place. "I know the recovery room is rough, but they'll be moving you to your room soon. Are you up to having a visitor?" She nodded. The doctor touched Judd on the shoulder. "Remember, only ten minutes. Don't get thrown out again."

Judd wasn't listening. His gaze was fixed on Stevie's face. He bent over her, careful not to dislodge any of the tubes. "I had to fight my way in here. I hope you appreciate it."

"How'd you find me?"

"I put Addison on your trail. I phoned him from a truck stop on the interstate. Ramsey wouldn't accept a collect call from me, the s.o.b., so I had to borrow change from the trucker I had hitched a ride with. He even felt so sorry for me that he bought me a cup of coffee, too. Turned out that he's based in Dallas and is an avid reader of my column. For his trouble, I promised him a season pass to the Mavericks' games."

She tried to follow the explanation, but it was far too complicated. "Addison?"

Smiling over her confusion, Judd said softly, "I'll tell you about it later. There's almost enough material there for another novel."

She tried to moisten her lips with her tongue, but her mouth was still too dry even though she had been allowed a few more ice chips. "Judd, what about my operation?"

He drew a more serious expression, leaned in closer, and when he spoke, it was in a raspy, confidential voice. "I might have known you were just showing off, pulling one of your cute-isms for the benefit of the crowd. Much ado about nothing."

"What was?"

"Your tumors. All those headlines and hoopla over a bunch of benign tumors." His tone was chastising, but there was a telltale moisture in his eyes.

"Benign?"

"Harmless little critters. Every last one of them."

She closed her eyes. Tears leaked from them. He brushed them away with the pad of his thumb. "They're sure?" she asked.

"If your gynecologist and the finest pathologist in Dallas know their stuff, it's a sure thing you're cured."

"Then they didn't have to do a hysterectomy?"

"If you discount your right ovary."

"They had to remove an ovary?"

He shrugged. "Inconsequential when you consider that everything else is intact and functioning. Oh, and while they were there, they took out your appendix. I told them I didn't think you'd mind."

"Judd," she whispered, tears of gladness bathing her cheeks.

"Hey, stop blubbering or that bitch of a nurse will have me kicked out again for disturbing the peace."

"You shouldn't have come."

"Those proverbial wild horses couldn't have kept me away."

Stevie sniffed back her tears. "I'm sorry I stole your car."

"What the hell? It really belongs to the bank more than it does to me anyway. Are you feeling okay?"

Laughing was out of the question, but she smiled. "I've got needles in my arm and hand, metal clamps holding my belly together, I can't even tee-tee on my own and I'm straddling an ice pack. They make me cough every so often, though I'm sure it rips out all my stitches. In short, I feel terrible."

"Not as terrible as I felt before I found out where you had gone. If you ever run out on me without an explanation again, I'll tan your hide."

She ignored the edict. "Did you write today?"

"Write?" he asked incredulously. "Stevie, I've been stalking the corridors of this hospital like a wild man waiting for you to come out of the anesthesia."

"You should've been home writing. Chapter seven needs work."

"Yeah, I know. It's dragging in—" He broke off. His eyebrows formed a fearsome V. "How in hell do you know what chapter seven needs?"

"I've been reading your novel."

"Since when?"

"Since you started it." She wanted to touch him badly, but couldn't find the wherewithal to raise her hand. "It's wonderful. Truly."

She felt the postoperative medication luring her back into oblivion. Before she succumbed, there was something she had to say. "Judd, I love you."

He took her hand and held it against his lips after pressing a fervent kiss on the backs of her fingers. "I figured that out when you decided to go for life instead of the Grand Slam. Want to know the real corker? I love you, too."

Smiling wryly, he realized that she'd drifted back to sleep. He regretted that she hadn't heard his first profession of love, but that was okay.

He would still be there when she woke up.

Epilogue

***

"Thank you."

"Thank *you*," the attractive young woman gushed. "I can't wait to read it. If it's half as good as your picture on the dust jacket, I'll be thoroughly entertained."

Judd glanced up at his wife, who was glaring at the gum-popping, high-strutting, miniskirted ingenue through slitted brown eyes. When they ventured back to her husband, he gave her a helpless shrug that was at odds with his smile, which defined masculine complacency.

"Mrs. Mackie, the line outside the door just keeps getting longer," the manager of the Manhattan bookstore said. "Mr. Mackie is going to be busy signing books for quite some time. Would you care to sit down?"

"I'm fine for now, but thank you."

He glanced at her shyly. "Would it be presumptuous of me to ask for your autograph, too."

"Not at all," she returned with a smile.

He produced a pad and pen. "I saw you play at the U.S. Open once."

"Did I win?"

"You lost in the quarter finals, but it was a close match."

Stevie only laughed.

"You're semiretired now, isn't that right?"

"I don't play competitive tennis anymore, but I'm busy organizing some instructional clinics."

"So I've heard. For underprivileged children, aren't they?"

After six months of recuperation following her surgery, her gynecologist had given her the go-ahead on any project she wanted to tackle.

Her brainstorm, which she had considered from every angle during her convalescence, had won Judd's hearty approval. He'd helped publicize the idea locally through his column in the *Tribune*. As a result, donations to support the project had poured in.

The original clinic in Dallas had received so many accolades that other cities had approached Stevie to organize similar programs for them. There were now Stevie Corbett Tennis Clinics nationwide, catering specifically to players who couldn't afford club memberships.

"The clinics are community supported and open to anyone who shows up wanting instruction," she said in response to the bookseller's question.

"Doesn't your husband mind sharing you with such a time-consuming undertaking?"

"Not at all. He understands my need to work. Besides, he's been busy himself."

"I understand that his daily column is now in syndication and that he's already at work on a second novel."

"That's right."

"What's it about?"

She gave the man a sweet smile. "I'm sworn to secrecy. You'll have to wait along with all his other fans."

There was a long line of them snaking out the door and down the sidewalk. Stevie watched as one elbowed his way through the crowd until he reached the table where Judd was autographing copies of his book. He introduced himself as a book editor for the *Times*.

"Can I have a minute, Mr. Mackie?"

"Nope," Judd said amicably, pointing down the line of people waiting to meet the author of the new best-seller. "But I can talk and sign at the same time. Ask away."

"Is the novel autobiographical?"

"Parts of it."

"Which parts?"

"In deference to my family and friends, I can't answer that question. I will admit that, as a young man, I wanted more than anything to play professional baseball. I was denied the chance. For years afterward, I harbored a lot of bitterness and carried a chip on my shoulder the size of Mount Everest." He closed the book he'd just signed, handed it to the customer and smiled a welcome to the next person in line. "Hi."

As he scrawled a brief message and his signature, he continued. "I was disenchanted with life, so I could relate to the protagonist in this book, who had also suffered a bitter disappointment."

"What changed your personal outlook?" the reporter asked.

Judd's gaze found Stevie's across the crowded bookstore. He saw her eyes shining back at him.

"I met somebody with real guts. She taught me through example that life is damn sure worth living even with all its drawbacks, and that sometimes we have to suffer a defeat in order to recognize a victory."

A sunny smile broke across Stevie's face. But it was immediately replaced by an expression of alarm. The alarm was telegraphed to Judd, who dropped his pen onto the table and left his position behind it.

He crossed the store in three strides and pressed his wife's hands between his. "Stevie, is something wrong?"

"Not at all, darling. Go back to work."

"Mr. Mackie," the bookstore manager said nervously, "people are waiting."

"I'll be right back," Judd told him, drawing Stevie down the narrow aisle toward the back of the store.

"But...but you can't leave now. Where are you going?" he sputtered. "What'll I tell the customers?"

"Tell them that I've been signing books for two hours and I have to take a leak. I'm sure they'll understand."

He left the bookseller, the reporter and those customers close enough to hear his statement gaping speechlessly as he pulled Stevie past the overloaded bookshelves into a rear storeroom that was even more cramped than the store proper.

"What's the matter?" he demanded the second the door closed behind them.

"Nothing."

"I saw your face, Stevie. You look like I do every time you playfully grab my—"

"Judd! People will hear you."

"I don't care. I want to know what brought on that expression that made you look like you'd just been goosed."

From the day they had returned to the east Texas farmhouse following her surgery, he constantly wanted to be apprised of the state of her health. Only after she'd had a normal menstrual cycle did he begin to believe the doctor's positive prognosis. But he had never totally relaxed his vigilance where her health was concerned.

"I knew I shouldn't have listened when you begged to come along today," he said now, berating himself for letting her persuade him. "Let me put you in a cab back to the hotel."

"Forget it, Mackie. I love watching people adore you, because I adore you so much myself." She gave him a soft kiss. "Besides, I refuse to stay cooped up in that stuffy little room while you're out getting ogled by every woman you meet."

"Not *every* woman," he replied with the insufferable conceit she now found so endearing.

She linked her arms around his neck and moved in close. "You're incorrigible. Why do I love you so much?"

"How can you help yourself? What's not to love?" Slipping his hands to the small of her back he drew her even nearer and angled his parted lips over hers.

"Mackie, you've got people waiting."

"Let them wait."

He kissed her thoroughly, using his tongue to search the sweet recesses of her mouth. Their hunger for each other hadn't abated a single degree. Judd often joked that he was probably the only husband in history who'd had to wait twelve weeks after the wedding to consummate his marriage. Stevie would retort that he had only himself to blame since he'd insisted on bringing a minister to the farmhouse to marry them while she was convalescing and that, once he'd gotten her gynecologist's okay, he had certainly made up for all the lost time.

"Hmm, delicious," he said now, lifting his lips off hers at last, "I've been craving—" He broke off suddenly. His expression went completely blank.

Stevie began to laugh softly. "Now who looks like he's been goosed?"

"What the hell was that?"

"That," she said, taking his hand and moving it down to her swollen abdomen, "is our baby, moving for the first time."

Judd's adam's apple slid up and down his neck when he swallowed hard. "Oh, Geez," he groaned, "I knew I should have insisted that you stay in the room. I knew this would be too tiring. Standing up on this damn hard floor brought this on. Why aren't you sitting down?"

Happiness bubbled out of her in the form of soft laughter. "Will you calm down? It's normal. It's right on time. The doctor told me on my last visit to be watching for movement. There it is again. Feel it?'' They waited expectantly, but nothing happened. ''I guess he went back to sleep.''

''Unfortunately,'' Judd said thickly, ''touching you has brought me wide awake.'' He nudged her with his middle so she couldn't possibly mistake his meaning. ''I'm a lucky cuss. Married to the sexiest prego broad on earth.''

''Have I ever told you that you really have a romantic way with words?''

''No.''

''Good.''

It was a word game they often played. He was smiling at her wit as his hands skimmed past her thickened waistline and moved up to her breasts. Over the past few weeks they'd grown larger with her advancing pregnancy. ''Tender?'' he asked as he massaged them through her dress.

''Not as long as you're doing that.''

He swept his thumbs across her nipples; they didn't disappoint him. ''God, I love you. You came along when I needed you most.'' He swallowed hard again, this time with emotion. ''Every time I think about your surgery and what could have been . . ." He let the unbearable thought go unspoken.

"But it wasn't, and we are blessed with each other." Again they kissed, putting behind it the love that brimmed in their hearts.

"Judd, it's happening again!" she said excitedly.

She guided his hand down to her tummy and they smiled radiantly at each other as the child of their creation moved within her.

"Does it hurt?" he whispered.

"No," she whispered back.

There was a knock on the door. "Mr. Mackie, the crowd is getting testy."

"What does it feel like?" Judd asked his wife, ignoring the panicked bookseller and keeping his voice low and stirring.

"It feels marvelous. It makes me feel alive and wonderful. Victorious. Almost as good as I feel every time you're inside me."

Judd laid his lips against hers and growled, "I've gotta go for now, Mrs. Mackie, but hold that thought."